PROMISED

KING BROTHERS BOOK FOUR

LISA LANG BLAKENEY

WRITERGIRL PRESS

LISA LANG BLAKENEY

Love reading novels featuring hot alpha men who fall for smart women? Then join MY VIP MAILING LIST at http://LisaLangBlakeney.com/VIP and get a **free** book just for joining!

Published by: Writergirl Press

FOLLOW ME

Follow me on Facebook
Join my Fan Group
Follow me on Amazon
Follow me on Bookbub

LICENSE NOTE

This book contains mature content, including graphic sex. Please do not continue reading if you are under the age of 18 or if this type of content is disturbing to you.

NOTE: All characters in the book are 18+ years of age, non-blood related, and all sexual acts are consensual.

To Every Reader Who Fell In Love With A King Brother...This is for you.

BOOKS BY LISA

The Masterson Series

Masterson

Masterson Unleashed

Masterson In Love

Joseph Loves Juliette

The King Brothers Series

Claimed

Indebted

Broken

Promised

The Nighthawk Series

Gunslinger

Wolf

Diesel

The Valencia Mafia Series

Rum Runners

INTRODUCTION

King Brother Drama.
King Brother Hotness.
A King Happily Ever After.

You are cordially invited to A King Family Wedding. The question is which one of the Kings will make it to the altar?

Follow these three badass brothers as they unapologetically claim their forever after in this short and sweet, sexy novella.

AUTHOR NOTE

While all of The King Brother books are interconnected standalone romances, this novella is unique in that it asks the question "what happened next" between each couple and who's going to make it to the altar (although you probably already have a good idea if you've read all three novels:). That's why it is best to read after this after you've enjoyed the other books in the series.

Important Timeline Notes:

Camden and Jade's story in this book falls **before the bonus epilogue** in their story, Claimed which fast forwarded the couple three years.

Cutter and Sloan's story in this book falls **after the epilogue** in their story, Indebted.

Stone and Ariana's story in this book falls **directly after** the end of their story, Broken.

SLOAN

A thin layer of sweat coats my body and the room reeks of sex. I push my hands firmly against a wall of dense muscle which is practically smothering me, in an effort to cool off, but to no avail. My man is heavy as hell and totally unmovable.

Cutter and I have been making love for approximately forty-five minutes, and I know this for sure because I was supposed to be in the shower exactly forty-five minutes ago. I'm meeting one of my clients in an hour for a discussion about a redecorating project of his office located in the Olde City section of the city. It's obvious that now I'm going to be late. My tardiness is beyond unprofessional, but as usual, my "king" wouldn't be denied.

At some point in the early morning I became hot and unconsciously slipped off my night tee, which left me wearing nothing but a sheer lavender thong. But my nakedness is like a beacon for Cutter. He can sense it in his sleep. With my eyes still closed, and his half open, I felt the thin strings of my thong being ripped to shreds and his head between my legs.

Ok, so maybe I'm blaming him for things that aren't one hundred percent his fault. Maybe I didn't take off my nightshirt accidentally, and perhaps it's very possible that I knew exactly what would happen when I did. So in actuality, I guess I'm the one guilty of initiating this particular little love making session this morning.

I attribute it to the fact that we have become recently engaged, and that I still must be on some sort of new fiancee high. It's nuts if you think about it. I didn't think I was the girlfriend type, much less the marrying type a few months ago. Yet here I am, promised to the last man on earth I'd expect to be.

My other theory on why I've jumped Cutter's bones this morning, the theory which actually makes the most sense, is the simple fact that he's a certifiable sex god. I've never admitted it out loud, because it's not like his enormous ego needs the accolades, but it doesn't matter.

He already knows.

I've never been this strongly attracted to a man, like I am to Cutter. I look at his huge, hard, chiseled body and blush almost every single time that I do (especially after he's jumped out of the shower).

When he tells a joke, I laugh hard. Like big belly laughs. I mean the guy is funny without even having to try hard. I can already tell when his top lip starts to hitch up in a certain way that he's about to say something funny. Sometimes I laugh before he's even started talking. That's why he tells me that he's marrying his number one fan, because I laugh at all of his jokes.

And just forget about it when this man gets excited. When Cutter gets fired up about something, I get excited. His enthusiasm is infectious. He loves people. He craves experiences. He enjoys life, and he makes me love it too.

Then when he tells me that I'm the most beautiful woman he's ever seen, I believe it. Thanks to my father, I have been in the local celebrity spotlight for most of my life. It isn't unusual for a local paper or blog to snap a shot of me at an event. And when they do, they often comment on what I'm wearing, how I look, and they do it in the most surface and shallow sort of way.

Yet when Cutter tells me I'm beautiful, that I'm his princess, it doesn't feel like just words or a shallow compliment. It feels true and genuine. Right down to the bottom of my soul, I believe every flattering remark that he's ever paid me.

And when he touches me.

Holy crap.

When he touches me I literally swoon. Sometimes his touch is delicate and reverent. Like he is worshiping every part of me. Then sometimes his touch is firm and frenzied. As if he needs to touch me to breathe, as if he needs to push and enter inside of me for survival.

Now if I was someone observing from the outside, I would talk all kinds of crap about what a tragedy I was. I would tell that woman to hand in her independent woman card, to hang her head in shame, and to get a freakin' life.

Yeah, I'm a total a walking hypocrite.

Some days I have a really hard time wrapping my head

around the fact that I have a ring on my finger; gifted to me by a man I couldn't even stomach a few months ago.

"Can you please get your big ass body off of me?" I jokingly say through a well satiated grin. "I'm blazing hot."

I let out a quick yelp as Cutter unexpectedly and effortlessly flips our positions in the bed. Now I'm laying on top of him. I try wriggling out of his grasp, but his strong hands hold me firmly in place.

"Yes, princess, you definitely are hot and speaking of asses–" He taps my butt with his hand then grabs one of my cheeks and jiggles it. "You ready for another round of this good lovin'?" he asks playfully.

"No, sir." I shake my head no. "I'm already late for my meeting."

"I love it when you call me sir," he jokes. His voice dripping with playful lust. "It sounds *so* right."

"I can't frolic with you anymore today," I chuckle.

"You sure? I'll do that thing with my tongue that you like."

"Uh-uh."

"I'll use an ice cube," he whispers seductively in my ear. "And the cuffs."

I drop my head in the crook of his neck and seriously consider his proposition for a moment. It's very tempting. That ice cube and cuff trick that Cutter does could weaken even the strongest woman's resolve. It's one of my favorites. Maybe I could stop working altogether and simply become his love slave.

"That's my girl," he croons as he begins to slide one of his thick fingers between my swollen folds. "You stay wet for me all the time, Princess. I love that about you among a million other things."

“What would those million other things be again?"

"What are you implying?" He grins. "You think I'm only interested in you for your body? This exquisite piece of art that bends and folds at my will and belongs only to me."

This is exactly why I'm late for my meeting. My legs, my pelvis, and my hips all seem to have a mind of their own right now. Cutter is playing my body like a fiddle, and it's responding instinctively. That is until I see the obnoxious green neon-colored numbers on his retro styled alarm clark out of the corner of my eye.

9:45am

I suddenly lift my head from his neck and clamp my legs together.

"I've got to go to work, lover. Seriously. Playtime is over."

He releases me and exaggerates a groan like he's in some sort of real physical pain.

"Ever since you quit your full time gig, I feel like you've been working more than you ever did. I'm seriously not understanding the point of it all."

I pick up my cell phone from the side table and send my client a brief but apologetic text.

Cutter is in rare form today. This is going to take at least another fifteen minutes.

CUTTER

"What is this the 1950's?"

I worship the ground that this long-legged, beautiful woman walks on, but right now I'd like to stuff a gag in her mouth, tie her to my bed, and fuck her well into the night. That would be my idea of a happy ending to this conversation. Alas, that would be entirely too easy.

Sloan has never been easy.

"No, princess. Neither of us were even born in the fifties," I deadpan.

"Exactly!" she says emphatically. "I know you're rich as sin, but I'm not like any of those little brats I grew up with in private school or the hordes of spoiled models and actresses you've slept with. I like to work. I want to work."

"And I want you to work, babe."

"But only if it isn't an inconvenience for you."

"I never said that."

Where the hell is my ball gag?

"You basically did."

"You're starting a fight for no reason other than to prove that you're right."

"I am right."

"No, babe, you're not."

"Do I say anything when you stroll in here at four or five am after you've been bouncing between the Tapas Lounge and the club all night? Smelling like smoke and minions."

Is she serious right now?

"No, but maybe that's because you *can't* say anything. You're right in there with me too, shaking your ass in the club every night."

"I'm in there some nights because when I'm there, I'm supporting your business," she says. Pointing her well manicured finger at me for emphasis. "Like a good girl-friend should."

"Let's face it. My *fiancee* is there for two reasons only." I make it a point to correct her. She is my fiancee, not my girlfriend, yet she continues to use the term a lot and it irritates the fuck out of me. "To keep an eye on me and the minions, and for the free drinks my bartenders keep comping you."

I actually love that Sloan is jealous. When we first met, she tried really hard to remain unaffected by everyone and everything. I suppose it was some sort of coping mechanism or a control thing. Like she had seen it and done it all. Seen one man, you've seen them all type of attitude. But that's not who my fireball is at all.

Sloan is territorial.

Sloan is jealous.

Sloan is possessive.

Sloan is my life.

"I'm sleeping with the owner." She mischievously grins. "Of course my drinks should be free."

"It doesn't seem like you're too interested in sleeping with the owner right now." I pout.

"Cutter freakin' King. I can't believe you. I'm an entrepreneur. Something which you encouraged me to pursue by the way. I cannot simply bail on a meeting whenever I feel like it. My interior design business is new, and it's basically a twenty-four hour hustle to get it off the ground. You should understand that. You're the greatest entrepreneur known to mankind right? God knows you never stop claiming that you are."

"Obviously I know what it takes to build a successful business," I say with restrained annoyance. "But your design work is second nature to you. It's your passion. Why do you have to spend hours holding meetings to convince these rich bastards to hire you? Your portfolio speaks for itself. I've told you a million times I can throw you a couple of clients that will keep you busy all year. No groveling necessary."

"I'm not groveling, and I rather book my own clients thank you very much."

Why does she have to make everything so difficult?

"What the hell for?" I gripe. "This business of yours is feeling too much like a job when it's supposed to be fun."

"I'm having loads of fun!"

"Well you seem to be the only fucking one."

"You're so spoiled. I swear. Why do I bother with you?"

Sloan tries to end the conversation by attempting to maneuver herself out of my grip, but she should know better. She can get up when I'm ready for her to get up.

"Obviously, I'm spoiled, darlin'. I'm a king."

"You're delusional."

"And hot."

"Puh-lease...and ridiculous."

"And the love of your life."

"Maybe," she teases.

"Maybe?" I grab her left hand. "This ice on your finger definitely confirms that I am."

"This?" she says indifferently.

Sloan stops trying to free herself from my grasp and holds her hand up to playfully glower at her engagement ring as if it's not much. It rubs me completely the wrong way, but I put faith in the fact that I know my girl.

"Yes– that." I playfully tickle her sides to lighten the mood.

"I hope that you realize that the size of this diamond is not some sort of accurate measure of our feelings, or our commitment for each other. It's just a ring."

I raise a curious eyebrow at that last statement.

Just a ring?

What the fuck is she talking about?

Sloan's poor choice of words seem to hang like a heavy funk in the air around us. We both are silent for what seems like an eternity, until I decide to diffuse the situation like I always do– with humor and sex.

"The size of this diamond might not be an indicator, but the volume of your orgasms are. You must love me lots, because they grow louder every time I'm inside of your pretty ass. Why don't we find out just how loud they can get right now?"

Then I pull out the big guns and tickle her under her arms.

SLOAN

"They are not loud!" I protest. Gasping for breath in between laughter. He's tickling me to death.

"My princess is a screamer."

"Stop!" I plead as I grab a hold of my tormenter's wrists and hold them down above his head on the bed (or rather he permits me to).

"Stop tickling me you neanderthal. You know I can't stand it," I say breathing heavily.

"Wait until you see what happens at the next tenant meeting. Watch the looks that you get from sweet old Mrs. Mason. She can hear you through the walls even when she turns up the television."

"You look positively thrilled about that."

"I don't mind everyone in the building knowing that I know how to keep my woman satisfied. In fact, I'm actually surprised that Kyle has never mentioned how good you're getting it. Isn't his bedroom on the other side of our living room wall?"

"This is not our living room wall. It's yours."

Cutter's face hardens.

This isn't our first conversation about our living arrangement or lack thereof. Cutter thinks it's ridiculous that I want to stay in my apartment which is just a few feet away from his. I just don't see it that way.

"A fact which can easily be remedied by you giving me the ok to rent out your apartment. You're never in it."

"You know how I feel about that."

"You feel things entirely too much. Get out of your feelings, and let's be practical about it instead."

I release his wrists and sit up.

"You're talking to me about being practical? That's unbelievable seeing as how you bought this entire building just to harass me."

"Correction, impress you."

"What's impressive or practical about buying a piece of real estate that you didn't need nor want?"

"It's called being romantic, Miss Pearson, and romance always trumps practicality. Any other woman–"

"Any other woman what?!" I interrupt defiantly.

"Any other woman would see what I meant by the gesture. Would be moved by the gesture. Would be creaming in her panties because of the gesture."

"Buying this building was over the top." I motion my hands around the room.

"I'm fucking over the top, Sloan!" he yells. "Why are you acting like you don't know who I am? Who I've always been. Who you fell in love with."

"You're right, I shouldn't have said that."

"That's right, you shouldn't have. As a matter of fact

there's a lot of things you shouldn't have said today, but I'm going to chalk that up to you not being a morning person."

I don't respond to that and simply roll my eyes at him.

"I bought you a ring and you said yes. We spend most of our time in this apartment. We're getting married this summer. There's no reason why you shouldn't just move in here officially. Especially because your unit could bring us in extra income. Fiscally it makes all the sense in the world."

"I'm not trying sound pretentious or anything, but you and I both know that you can afford to keep that apartment vacant for the next twenty years and it wouldn't affect your bottom line. You don't need the money. You're loaded."

"And good business decisions will help keep it that way."

I slap him playfully in his abs and move to get off of him and out of the bed. I'm finished with all this discussion of moving in together. Things are fine just the way they are. I like knowing that I have my own apartment just in case I need or want my space, and I'm not budging on that, at least until we get married.

"Stay where you are, Mrs. King."

Cutter pulls me tenderly by the wrist and back down into his rock hard body.

"It's still Miss Pearson. I'm not your wife quite yet."

I kiss him softly on the cheek, and partially on the corner of his mouth. I love how his eyes close when I do this. As if my kiss is a soothing balm for his soul. As if my kiss is everything.

"That's why our friends are throwing us an engagement versus an anniversary party tonight," I tell him. "A party which you better be at on time. No excuses."

"Why do we have to pretend like this is a surprise again?"

"Because I'm sure that Elizabeth didn't anticipate that your brother and your best friend would gossip to you about the party like two little ten year olds. It'll ruin everything if we don't act like we're surprised. She worked so hard."

"It was kind of silly for her to think that she could keep anything a surprise from me. Cam is my brother and my best friend. He tells me everything. Everybody knows that."

"Umm, well he doesn't tell you everything."

"Like what?"

"Oh how soon we forget," I taunt. "You practically disowned your beloved older brother when you found out that he didn't tell you about Stone."

"You mean he didn't mention the possibility of Stone's existence. He didn't know for sure."

"Tomato, Tamato."

"That's not funny, Princess. Why are you bringing that old shit up?"

"I'm not trying to be funny, and it's not that old. It literally just happened."

"It's over."

"Okay, I'm just saying...your brother doesn't tell you everything."

"You said that shit already."

"Sheesh, you're touchy. I thought you'd come to terms

with the fact that Camden knew about your long lost brother before you did."

"Like I said, Camden didn't actually know anything which is why he didn't say anything. It's over and I have come to terms with it. Speaking of Stone, was he invited to this so-called surprise engagement party of ours tonight?" he asks in an almost accusatory tone as if Stone would be left out on purpose.

"Of course he was."

"How do you know that he was if the party is a secret."

"No one is leaving Stone out of anything, Cutter. Relax. Elizabeth wouldn't do that."

"I just want to make sure that he feels included."

"You mean you want me to make sure that I include the man that was lying and stealing from one of my best friends?"

"That's bullshit and you know it. There were extenuating circumstances."

"Tiny threw him out of her house."

"And now they live in another house together. Like two little love birds."

"I'll never understand it."

"If she's figured out a way to forgive him, so can you."

"Well that goes both ways. Tonight is going to be a great night for you to bond with Tiny. So please be on your best behavior."

"What do you mean bond with her?"

"You know very well that she's one of my best friends, and is in love with *the new brother,* yet you've only exchanged about ten words with her."

"That's not true."

"It's totally true."

"It's not my fault she doesn't talk."

"No one can get a word in edgewise when you're in the room."

"Yet, it's amazing how you always seem to have plenty to say." Cutter grins.

"Just figure it out, wise ass, because if Tiny doesn't give you the best friend seal of approval, I may have to reconsider marrying you."

CUTTER

"Is that a threat?" I ask giving Sloan a careful glance. With every semi-fucked up thing she's said this morning, I'm not completely sure whether or not we're still playing around.

"It's a promise," she says with mischief in her eyes.

Okay, we're still playing.

That's more like it.

"So if I agree to win her over tonight will you be nicer to me right now?" I ask suggestively.

"You know I'd love to but seriously I can't." She kisses me dismissively on the lips. "I've already texted my client the hugest lie ever as an excuse for pushing back the meeting."

"Who are you meeting with again?"

"A lawyer named Edward Prentis. This is actually our second meeting."

"You mean Eddie 'lazy eye' Prentis?"

Sloan sighs with exasperation.

"Don't tell me you know him."

"He's a partner over at the Provident Law Group right?"

"Oh my god! Do you know every man under forty years old on this planet?"

"Not everyone, darlin', but I definitely know everyone in Philadelphia, and within a fifty mile radius of it. This is my town. Camden and I practically raised ourselves in these streets, and we've met a lot more people as fixers."

"So in other words, you know Mr. Prentis, and there's something about him that you don't particularly care for."

I hate that Sloan calls Prentis mister anything. He doesn't deserve the respect. This is exactly why I wish she would just take my referrals. I know of several businesses that would hire her strictly for her commercial design skills. Not just to get into her panties. Which is Prentis's total MO.

"Yeah, I don't particularly care for the fact that he's a dick."

"Well I'm never going to get any work if I have to avoid every man who you think is a dick."

Eh, maybe she's right.

"Just work for women then," I suggest.

"That's a terribly ignorant thing to say."

"You're right. I bet there's a shit ton of women who'd like to sleep with you too given the chance. So how about you just redecorate the club then? Only work for me. That'll keep things super simple."

"You're certifiable. You know that right?"

Powerful pheromones are flying all over the room. The scent of me all over Sloan is wafting inside of my nostrils, making me want her again in the most primal sort of way. I just want to pull her back into bed and make love to her for another hour.

And another.

And another.

Good thing I'm marrying this woman because I'm definitely addicted to being inside of her. It's my favorite place on earth.

"I know, darlin'. That's why you love me."

"I can't redesign the club. It was just redecorated."

"Yeah– but I bet you could make it look even sexier."

I began to knead the muscles of Sloan's beautifully, toned thighs. Hoping she'll finally break down and ditch the meeting with 'lazy eye' Prentis.

"I bet I could," she says smiling at me. "But that's not the point. That would be a total waste of your money. Plus that's just your way of keeping an eye on me. Why you think every man in the world wants to sleep with me is beyond me."

"Because they do."

"Cutter–"

Sloan is all woman. She likes to put on makeup and a nice dress when she goes out, but truly has no idea how totally stunning she is. I haven't met a man yet that hasn't given her a second look or a third when she walks in a room. Sometimes they look so hard at her that they make my eyelid twitch, which is never a good thing. It means that I'm probably getting ready to beat somebody's ass.

"You literally have thousands of Instagram followers, and a huge percentage of them are men. Men who like every post and reply with weird fucking emojis. They're probably jacking off to your pictures right now."

"Well first of all, it's weird that you've been stalking my Instagram account, so stop it. Second of all, you know many of those guys follow me because they're intrigued with anything having to do with my father."

"They're not liking pictures of your long legs and big ass in a short dress because of your father."

"Oh, stop it. It's not like I ever met a man through social media. The truth is I hadn't been on a decent date in months, before I started seeing you."

I prop myself half up in the bed with a pillow and position her straddled across my lap.

"Do you really think that was because the dating gods had it out for you?" I chuckle.

"Probably, I was in a huge slump."

She's so stinking cute.

"No, my love. You're not that unlucky. That was completely all of my handiwork."

"Wait...what?"

SLOAN

My mouth forms the most perfect round o shape.

I'm shocked.

I'm engaged to a saboteur.

Elizabeth's fiance (Roman) mentioned something about this to me a long time ago, but I dismissed it because I thought he was messing with my head. The two of us kind of have a love-hate relationship with each other.

Plus I didn't think it was possible for anyone to interfere in my love life like that, nor did I understand what Cutter's motivation would be. I always believed that he thought of me as strictly Elizabeth's best friend and nothing more.

He never showed any interest in me. In fact, he barely said two words to me when I would go to the club. He was too busy holding court with all his other women, or as I (not so) fondly call them, his mindless minions. Club sluts that happily do his bidding.

"How?"

"It was easy," he said. "I just cocked blocked."

"Explain," I say. Demanding a more detailed answer than that.

"I simply had a few gentle conversations with whatever man tried to get into your panties. So needless to say, I was having a lot of those conversations. You're a very popular girl, Princess. No surprise there. You're intoxicating."

"That would actually be kind of sweet if it wasn't so crazy. Were you a bully in high school or something? I can't believe you just go around threatening people for fun."

"Who said anything about bullying? I told you. I had a few gentle conversations with the dudes. I was doing you a favor. They were all douchebags anyway."

He starts playing with my nipples. Knowing that's my number one weakness. I take the tiniest gasp of pleasure but try and stay focused on the conversation at hand. He's clearly deflecting.

"I've never heard or seen you do anything gentle in your life," I say.

"What did we just do this morning? That was gentle."

I grab his hands to stop them from playing with me.

"You fucked me."

"Uh, uh, uh. I made sweet love to you."

"There was nothing sweet about it."

He chuckles. "It was very sweet."

"It was rough and dirty. It's always rough and dirty."

"I didn't tie your ass up to this bedpost, so it was sweet by my standards." He attempts to sound a little offended, but I know better. There isn't much that can offend Cutter, especially when it comes to his sexual performance. He's quite confident about his skills in the bedroom.

"Exactly...your standards are highly questionable. But make no doubt about it, my liege." I kiss him firmly on his mouth and he moans softly. "I love every little dirty moment, but now I've really got to get to work."

I catch Cutter off guard and leap off of him, practically running out of the room towards the shower. He's the kind of man who has a difficult time taking no for an answer, so sometimes you just have to take matters into your own hands. I can't help but laugh when not even three minutes later I hear the bathroom door handle jiggling.

"Sloan!" I hear him roar.

Cutter loves to have shower sex, and any other day I do too, but we just don't have the time. I'm beyond late.

"Open this fucking door!" he commands.

"Oh did I lock it?" I laugh as I turn on the water.

"That's not funny, Sloan."

"I don't have time for any shower games with you. A good fiance would support his woman and not try to sabotage her career."

"You already cancelled the appointment, so you might as well stay in with me."

I hear the knob jiggling some more. Harder this time.

"You better not break that doorknob, Cutter. That's a custom piece I ordered for you, not some mass market made knob from the neighborhood hardware store. And I didn't cancel my appointment, I just pushed it back."

The jiggling stops.

Finally he's given up.

Good.

In my text, I rescheduled with Edward and told him that I'd meet him in ninety minutes at my favorite coffee shop, Java The Hut. As long as traffic is good, and the meeting stays on track, I'll still have plenty of time afterwards to pick up a new dress for tonight and get my hair done by party time.

I'm right in the middle of washing my private parts when I hear a clicking sound. I can't see much due to the fog clouding the glass of the shower door, but I notice the large silhouette entering the bathroom and placing what appears to be some sort of dark colored credit card on the counter.

It can't be.

"Did you just jimmy the bathroom lock with your American Express Black Card?" I ask incredulously.

Cutter's heavy barefooted steps continue to silently walk across the tiles of the bathroom floor with purpose. I feel an instant rush of cool air as the shower door whips open, and I stare slack-jawed at the man standing on the other side of it in all his naked glory.

I know I get to see him everyday, but the magnificence of Cutter's nude body is something to behold. It takes my breath away each and every time I look at him. Not an ounce of fat on him. Shoulders so strong and sculpted that it's no wonder how they've effortlessly lifted me into all sorts of small places and strange positions. A perfect six pack that trails into a well cut V which points to my favorite piece of his anatomy. Yeah, there's no doubt about it. I'm a lucky girl.

"Can I help you?" I ask sarcastically as my body reacts to him like the double-crosser it is. My nipples turn as hard as the diamond on my finger.

Cutter licks the corner of his mouth while staring directly at my breasts, then down at the washcloth in my hand (especially where it's positioned), then looks back at me with the huge grin that I've grown to love.

"You won't be needing this, Princess." He drops to his knees and snatches the washcloth out of my hand. Tossing it against the tiled wall. Then closing the shower door behind him. "I've taken the liberty of pushing your meeting back with Eddie another hour. He won't mind."

"You're insufferable," I groan as my head falls back in pleasure against the granite tiles.

"Yes I am," he says smugly. "And you're welcome."

SLOAN

My mother was a rare beauty in her heyday. Actually she still is. Long legs, stunning eyes, natural blonde waves, and curves in all the right places. My father was a highly skilled professional athlete with a rock hard body, beautiful coffee brown skin, and a smile that notoriously broke hearts.

So I've grown up always being told just how genetically blessed I am, because I supposedly received the best of the two of them. I've also been really careful not to believe any of that except for today.

Today I believe every word.

Today, for a moment, I feel like an actual American princess.

And it only took a very pregnant Elizabeth to practically threaten me with bodily harm to get me here.

"That dress looks amazeballs on you, Sloan. You look like a Grecian goddess. That's the one. That's the dress you should walk down the aisle in!" she exclaims as she rubs her swollen, pregnant stomach like it's a crystal ball.

I'm standing on an elevated platform in front of a set of mirrors, doing a pirouette in a wedding dress made of a gauze-like Italian silk. The fourth dress Elizabeth has bullied me into trying on over the last thirty minutes.

I'm not supposed to be here today. In fact I'm supposed to be shopping for a completely different dress. Preferable a short, eggplant-colored one for the "surprise party" that Elizabeth is throwing Cutter and me tonight–but of course I'm not supposed to know anything about that.

"It is kind of pretty, isn't it?" I ask quietly.

"It's not just pretty. It's stunning. I mean you'd look good in a paper bag, but this is different. It looks even better on you because of how you feel in it. I can tell that you love yourself in it."

I spin around once more for good measure. I really do like the dress, but I'm nervous about committing to it for a lot of reasons I can't explain or understand.

"It's definitely pretty, but I'm not going to buy the first dress I try on."

"This isn't the first one you tried on."

"No, but this is the first bridal shop I've been to."

"Have you two set a date yet?"

"No, Bitsy. Sheesh. I just got engaged."

"I thought Cutter didn't want to wait."

"This isn't just Cutter's decision."

"Uh-huh." Elizabeth sounds unconvinced. "So you don't want the dress."

"I have to shop around. Maybe we could even see a few in Paris after the baby is born."

Elizabeth's eyes enlarge.

"Wedding dress shopping in Paris? After the baby's born?! I didn't realize you were planning on such a long engagement."

"You're so big, you could probably drop that baby right in this dressing room. We actually won't have to wait that long."

Elizabeth shakes her head as if she's annoyed with me.

"What?" I say. "I just don't want to make any hasty decisions. This is hopefully a once in a lifetime moment, so I want to pick the perfect dress."

"That dress is perfection."

"I'm going to keep looking."

"Don't tell me you're going to be one of *those* brides, because I'm way too pregnant to put up with any of your perfection seeking, alpha girl tendencies."

Elizabeth winces as she shifts her swollen body in the sitting room chair.

"You better not be having contractions," I fuss.

I quickly step down off of the platform and prop her swollen ankles up on a spare chair in our private changing room.

"I'm not having contractions, crazy girl. I'm just uncomfortable."

"Your feet look like little flotation devices. If this is what pregnancy looks like, I'm not in any rush to have any little Kings."

"Thanks a lot."

Sometimes I speak without thinking.

I've got to work on that.

"You're beautiful though. There's definitely some truth to the whole pregnancy glow theory."

She smiles at my effort to clean up my faux pas.

"That's what Roman says all the time. I don't see it." She shifts in her seat again and smiles. "I can't wait for this little love bug to come out. We're ready to meet him or her."

Elizabeth is pregnant with her first child and my first godchild. I proudly designed the baby's nursery, and now it's just a matter of time before he or she arrives. She will be the first mother in our small, but tight, circle of friends.

I am genuinely happy for her, but I think she may be forcing this bridal shop visit and the surprise party tonight, because she wants to pack all the things on her checklist in that she can before the baby comes. She has to know that once baby Masterson is born that Roman will put her on lockdown. She probably won't see the light of day until the baby is damn near one year old, if he has it his way.

"Does the dark knight (my nickname for Roman) know that you're out gallivanting around bridal shops with me today? You probably should be home resting."

"Putting my feet up at home is the same as placing them up in here. Plus you and I both know that if I didn't get the ball rolling, you wouldn't have ever started dress shopping."

"There's no rush."

"What's the wait?"

"I'm engaged aren't I?"

"An engagement is a precursor to a wedding for most couples."

"You're one to talk. Someone in this room seems to be doing things a little out of order and it ain't me."

"Really, Sloan? You sound so antiquated. Just like my mother and Aunt Juliette."

"Well they weren't totally off base. You're like a hundred weeks pregnant, living in sin, and not even close to being married either."

"I'm not going to marry the man of my dreams, while I'm nine months pregnant, just because it will make my mom and dad look like good parents in the eyes of their friends."

"You could have married Roman when you first found out you were pregnant. It's not like he would have complained."

"I'm not rushing my wedding for any frackin' body!"

"Ohhhh, is that right? Now I guess you understand what I'm saying. There's no freaking rush."

"Ugh, you're so annoying. Stop trying to get me all riled up to prove some sort of ridiculous point. You're upsetting my baby."

"No, you're upsetting *our* baby by talking so badly to it's Godmother."

Elizabeth rolls her eyes in annoyance. I can't help but crack a smile. I take pride in the fact that no one can annoy my bestie better than I can.

"Maybe Tiny is up for the position then."

"You better not, Elizabeth Hill. I called Godmom dibs on that baby before you even met Tiny. Your first baby was always supposed to be my godchild. There's no going back on that promise."

The matronly bridal assistant, who refers to herself as Miss Alberta, enters the room. She's an older woman with thick upper arms and thighs who dyes her gray hair entirely too jet black for her age, but sweet as pie and reminds me of one of my favorite aunts on my father's side of the family.

"How are we doing in here ladies?"

"Perfect," Elizabeth replies while at the same time I say, "Not so good."

"Oh no?" She looks back and forth between us with genuine concern. "How can I help?"

"There are so many beautiful dresses in here that I just can't make any sort of final decision right now," I say.

That's my subtle way of letting her know that I'm not buying anything today, and that she should probably move on to another actual paying bride in the showroom area.

"Aah, that's a common problem. When's the wedding?"

"Soon," Elizabeth interjects while at the same time I say, "The date is undecided."

Elizabeth turns up one side of her mouth and returns to rubbing her belly. Miss Alberta looks at both of us curiously but continues on with her questions.

"So tell me, the last time you envisioned your wedding day, what kind of dress did you see yourself in?"

She's not going to let me off easy.

"I've never had an exact vision per say of my wedding day. I mean is that a thing? Do women have visions?"

I can feel Elizabeth's judgmental stare searing the side of my face.

"Are you newly engaged?" Miss Alberta asks.

"Yes." I politely smile. "It hasn't been that long."

"Are you feeling a few jitters?"

"Umm, not really."

Elizabeth purses her lips in a tight smile. As if she's dying to call me a big fat liar but has decided wisely against it.

"Well, no matter. I can already tell what type of bride you are. Modern but understated. Nothing too obvious, too glamorous, too sexy or too pouffy. You need elegant, sleek, classic. A dress that skims the body."

"Which is exactly the type of dress that she has on right now," Elizabeth chimes in. "A classic. Like Meghan Markle's."

"Try this."

I'm not exactly sure where she whipped it out from, but Miss Alberta places a short and delicate wedding veil on top of my head. The length just meets the tip of my chin.

"It's perfect with this dress isn't it?"

I take another look at myself in the mirror and see only part of what the two of them both see. A beautiful dress. Me in a beautiful dress. Yet something in my gut is telling me not yet. To wait.

Sometimes you know something is coming. Something powerful. Something completely out of your control. You can feel it in the air. And you know that there is absolutely nothing you can do about it.

It's this very feeling that has been gnawing at my gut recently. I'm not sure when it started. I just woke up one day with an uneasy feeling on my heart. I've been ignoring it for days now, actually weeks, but it's getting much more difficult to do.

Elizabeth asks Miss Alberta in the most polite way to give us a few moments alone. As soon as she exits the room, the questions begin.

"What's wrong?"

"Nothing." I start maneuvering myself out of the dress and veil.

"Are you and Cutter ok?"

"We're better than ok."

"Then what is it? You're acting like a very reluctant bride and you're making me nervous."

The dress pools at my feet.

"Relax. Everything's fine."

"Good grief your boobs are perfect. You sure you never had them done?"

I ignore that thinly veiled compliment and consider the original question. What is up with me?

"I think...I think that I'm just waiting for the other shoe to drop."

"What do you mean?"

"I have this great guy. This new career. My best friends are happy in their relationships and there's a new baby on the way. I'm just not used to everything being this good. I've told you how I grew up. I never wanted for material things, but there was lots of instability in my home. If it wasn't one thing, it was another living in the Pearson house. In fact the one thing I've learned is that nothing stays this good forever."

"I've known you for years and I had no idea that you were this pessimistic, Sloan."

I step out of the dress and hold it up against my body with my hands. It smells new and the fabric feels expensive and cool against my skin. It would be a great dress for a summer wedding.

"Neither did I."

A wedding that for some reason I just can't seem to picture.

My phone dings.

My sister Dawn has forwarded me a link to a news article with a message from her that simply reads...

Call Me.

CAMDEN

"This party blows."

I laugh at my sweet little assistant. My lover. My best friend. She's been in a hell of a mood these last few days, and partying tonight with our friends and family was one of the last things she felt like doing– even if it is for Cutter (whom she adores).

I'm not sure what's going on with her but she's in a shitty way. If she wasn't on the pill, I would swear that Jade was pregnant with my child, or maybe that's just wishful thinking.

"You're just in a bad mood."

She leans in and tries lowering her voice. Something she actually should have done ten seconds ago. I'm sure a couple of Sloan's former co-workers just heard Jade complain about being at her own boss's engagement party. Not a good look.

"Are you paying attention?" she asks me rhetorically. "Look at Elizabeth. Look at Sloan. They're smiling with their mouths, but their eyes are saying something completely different. And look at Cutter. He's smiling and laughing so much that it's obvious he's hiding something."

"You're overstating things as usual, Nancy Drew. Elizabeth is damn near ten months pregnant and is about to pop any second, so of course she's miserable; and the glamazon ... well that's just her resting bitch face; and my brother is being who he is... class clown...life of the party."

"It's probably a very good thing you have me in your life, because you don't understand women at all. There's something else going on. Maybe you're right about Cutter, but those two are just going through the motions."

I've had two Jack and Coke highballs already, so maybe I'm a little off my game, but I don't see what Jade thinks she sees. What I do know is that if there's any inkling of truth to it, that liquor will solve all of that shit. Well at least for everyone except Elizabeth. She'll have to settle for something non-alcoholic and maybe an order of our famous wings.

"Marco is lining up lemon drop and kamikaze shots on the bar top," I announce. "Grab one or two please. Elizabeth, there's a shot of orange juice up there for you."

Cutter grabs the shot of OJ to give to Elizabeth.

"Aww, damn. Orange juice? I thought I read somewhere that pregnant women in Europe get to drink red wine if they want."

Roman snatches the shot glass out of my brother's hand.

"We're not in fucking Europe," he grumbles as he hands Elizabeth the shot of OJ and kisses her on the neck.

I grab Jade by the waist, pulling her into my side, and hand her a lemon drop.

"Here you go, itty bitty."

She holds her palm up to stop me.

"I think I ate something rancid for lunch. I better pass."

I don't like how there's something not quite right with my girl. I'm going to drag her ass in for a physical at somebody's doctor's office this week. No excuses this time.

"You want a glass of ginger ale to settle your stomach?"

"Yeah, I'll try that."

"Okay, and if that doesn't make you feel any better we can make our apologies and leave. Cutter will understand if you're not feeling well."

"You fuss too much, *grandma*. I'll be fine. Go give your brother the toast he deserves. This night is about those two love birds. Not me."

Damn, I love this woman.

Always such a trooper.

I rap on the bar top with my knuckles to gain everyone's attention.

"I'd like everyone to raise their shot glasses to my little brother and the woman of his dreams, the glamazon."

Jade elbows me in the waist and gives me a stern look. She warned me all day about calling Sloan anything other than her "government name".

"I mean Sloan."

Everyone laughs at my correction. Everyone but Sloan. Maybe she actually is pissed that I call her that. I never gave a shit about it before, but I suppose I need to change my ways since she is about to become family.

"Congratulations on your engagement Sloan and Cutter, and may the two of you drive each other completely insane like the rest of us do to each other."

I turn my eyes towards Jade.

The crowd laughs again.

Then Jade jabs me in the side once more and comments under her breath. "This isn't an episode of Saturday Night Light Live. Leave the jokes to the professionals."

"I was about to get to the serious part," I say in her ear. Inconspicuously nibbling her lobe for good measure.

I turn back to my audience.

"But seriously though... Cutter has waited a long time for you, Sloan. He knew you were special the moment he first spotted you when we were barely teenagers sneaking into the stadium to watch your dad play, and it looks like he got it right. You make my brother happier than I've ever seen him, and I wish you both nothing but the best in the future. Welcome to the family. Kings love hard, and Kings love long. Cheers!"

"Cheers!!" The room says in unison.

When the music cuts back on I turn to Jade.

"Did that meet your impossible standards of a good toast?"

"It took you a couple of tries but you did good, King. Cut looks happy."

"I didn't just do good, I rocked that shit."

"Whatever you need to believe."

I almost laugh at Jade's last snarky comment, when I notice that her eyes look a little dull to me, and that she hasn't taken a sip of her ginger ale the entire time that we've been standing here. She's just holding it in her hand.

"Did you have some?" I ask referring to the soda.

"I did."

"It doesn't look like it."

"I took a sip not a gulp."

"You want to leave?"

"No, Camden. I swear to you I'm fine. Just tired."

"You're not fucking fine."

"I'm not at a hundred percent, but I'm good enough to ride out this party."

"Hey, lima bean," Cutter interrupts and gives Jade a hug. "You're looking a little green around the gills. You had a rough night last night? Was Marco making you taste test one of his new drink concoctions again?"

"You two Kings are going to give me a complex. Do I look that bad? I'm fine, alright!"

Cutter leans his head back in an exaggerated way as if she just smacked him.

"Well, damn, you little stinky lima bean, I was just asking. Did my brother do something to piss you off? If he did, I'll shoot him in the pinky toe for you."

She almost laughs at that one.

"Congratulations on the engagement."

"I think you almost mean that."

"I do mean it," Jade offers. "I'm happy for you both."

"So then how about a double wedding for the King brothers. That shit would be awesome! Top shelf open bar. Seafood and steak sit down dinner. Get a couple of live acts for the entertainment. It will be the event of the summer. Everyone will want to be there!"

Waves of excitement and joy roll off of my brother in a very disingenuous way. Jade was right. He's way too hyped. There's something wrong but whatever it is, he doesn't want it to spoil the party.

It's hard for me not to ask him what it is and try and fix it for him. It's what I've done our entire lives. He's my little brother. I've always had his back. But he's starting a new life with the glamazon, and I'm going to have to respect that they will have their own problems and secrets that I won't be privy to unless Cutter chooses to share. Right now he isn't.

"Let's not get ridiculous," I say in an effort to play along with his act. "I don't think your fiancee would want a double wedding."

"What makes you say that?"

"I just can't see her family allowing another bride to take some of the shine away from their daughter's big day. She's the daughter of Dan Pearson. They're definitely going to pull out all the stops when she gets hitched."

"Honestly, it's a little weird that you want a double wedding anyway, Cutter. You two aren't twins," Jade chimes in.

"It's economical, you crab apple," Cutter retorts.

"Don't talk to my woman like that," I growl playfully.

"She's my assistant!"

"Correction, she's my woman first and *our* assistant second."

Jade laughs at the two of us, but I can see a slight pained look in her eyes when she does. Evidently everyone is hiding something tonight. That's my cue to exit.

I slap a hand on one of my brother's shoulders.

"Hey, Cut, Jade and I need to head out early. Make our apologies to the group. I don't feel like taking another fifteen minutes to say goodbye to everyone in here. Love you, little brother."

Cutter takes another careful look at Jade, and I know immediately that he sees it too. "No problem. Thanks for coming. I love your sentimental ass too. You too, Jade."

And the fact that Jade is no longer protesting that we're making an early exit tells me everything I need to know.

Something is incredibly off.

JADE

I've finally figured out why I've been feeling like crap for days. These boys are running me ragged. Every time I turn around one of them needs something, wants something, requires something. They're like children. Muscular, wealthy, spoiled children.

Today they're holding some sort of meeting that I, of course, have to sit in on. I honestly don't feel like it today, but if I don't start acting like everything is okay, my boyfriend is going to fly in a fucking infectious disease specialist or something. I love him, but Camden is turning into a freakin' worry wart.

If it sounds like I'm complaining, I'm not. There isn't a minute that goes by that I don't understand that this is what happiness looks like. I work for three young millionaires who treat me like family, and one of them would move heaven and earth for me– in and out of bed.

Seriously, some higher being took pity on my sad little life and put Camden King in my orbit, and I will forever be grateful.

When I get to Roman and Elizabeth's house, I text Roman to let him know that I'm outside. Might as well get used to a routine where I don't ring any doorbells and wake a sleeping baby, because that's how it's going to be when Elizabeth finally delivers.

"Hey."

"Hey."

"Why didn't you just ring the doorbell?"

"Sleeping baby."

Roman raises an eyebrow.

"You are so damn weird sometimes. There is no sleeping baby in here yet."

"There will be. So I'm just getting you in the habit of what to do. Where is your beloved by the way?"

"Doing something in the nursery. I'm not really sure what there's left to do though. The glamazon finished decorating the room weeks ago."

"Oh that's normal. She's nesting."

"What the hell is nesting?"

"You didn't read the book, did you?"

I'm referring to the baby bible, *What To Expect When You're Expecting,* and while I'm no expert on raising kids, even I know that it's the go-to reference for all new parents.

"Elizabeth has it covered."

"It's the holy grail of baby books. Just read it and maybe you can be of some help to her when the baby comes."

"I don't have time to read that big ass book."

"Forgive me...that's right...you're too busy calling random meetings."

"This one is important. I've got big news."

"Don't you always."

"Where is Cam by the way? Why didn't you two come together?"

"He had to make a stop."

I find Elizabeth exactly where Roman said she'd be. Curled up in the new oversized rocking chair in the nursery with her laptop and some healthy snacks by her side.

"Hey, Jade," she greets me brightly.

"How are you feeling today, prego? I see you're drinking your green juice and apple slices as I advised."

"I was but I can't drink any more of it. I feel like a stuffed pig."

"Good thing you don't look like one then isn't it?" I smile.

"That's easy for you to say with your flat stomach and normal sized breasts and feet. Mine feel like flotation devices. Especially after the party. I think I may have eaten a few too many salty things."

I hold in my laughter. It wouldn't be nice. Her feet do look like little overinflated animal balloons.

"Is Roman being helpful at least?"

"Yes– and overprotective and excited."

"Roman gets excited?"

Elizabeth chuckles. "Sure he does. Over certain things."

My mouth spreads wide for a big yawn.

"You seem tired."

"I think my allergies are bothering me."

"You have allergies?"

"Off and on."

I haven't had to really deal with my allergies since I changed what I eat a few years ago to a more plant based diet, but at this point it's pretty natural for the lies to fly out of my mouth. It's easier that way. I'm not used to having so many people concerned about my well-being like this.

"I don't know why Roman made the meeting this early. Didn't you have a long night at the club last night?"

Exhausting.

"Just the usual."

BECAUSE I ROLLED out of bed at the very last minute, I didn't get a chance to go on a run this morning. When I don't exercise or eat something colorful in the morning, I feel out of sorts. So while I wait on all of the Kings to arrive and assemble in the meeting room, I blend us all some smoothies. Thankfully Roman and Elizabeth employ a woman who keeps the place clean and stocks the fridge with fresh vegetables and the freezer with frozen fruit.

After I hand Camden his green smoothie, he winds his arm around one of my thighs and motions for me to sit down close to him.

"You alright, baby?"

Dammit, I'm going to have to really consider wearing some eye concealer or something. How does he always know that I'm tired?

"Fine." I rub and squeeze one of his tight shoulder muscles. "Now relax and drink your smoothie."

"Stop ordering me around," he grins. "In here, I'm the boss."

"In here. At home. In bed," I mutter flatly under my breath.

He grins sinisterly.

"I'm glad we have a mutual understanding."

JADE

When new brother (Stone) walks into the room, some of the levity floating in the air around us all is sucked out of the atmosphere. While Camden and Cutter have been quick to accept this new person into our circle of crazy; Roman, Sloan and I have been a little more cautious about it.

We all love Camden and Cutter in different ways. As a brother. As a lover. But the bottom line is that we all would do anything for those boys. I know for me, my reluctance to fully accept Stone has a lot to do with the brothers' past. They both have seen more than their fair share of grief and loss, and I don't want to see a look of disappointment cross either of their faces if Stone lets them down. Correction, when he lets them down.

While I don't usually hold my tongue in front of Camden (or anyone for that matter), the three of us have been especially careful about what we say in front of Tiny about Stone.

Somehow this dude has pulled a Jedi mind trick on her and made her fall in love with him in record time. Even after all the slimy shit he was trying to pull on her father, she's forgiven him and is living with him. I swear. *New brother* must have one powerful ass dick.

"Welcome, brother," Cutter says to Stone. "Have a seat at the table."

Stone doesn't say much. Another thing that annoys the hell out of me. I mean he's brand new on the scene. Who the hell is he to act all reserved and cautious. So what he's done time. My cousin Joey did some time too. He isn't a mute. In my opinion, Stone should have his guard completely down. Reveal to us who he really is if he wants our acceptance.

"I have some news," Roman says breaking the awkward pause in the room. "Miami is dead."

"What?!" We all collectively exclaim.

The boys are professional fixers. Cleaning up the messes that celebrities or other wealthy people get themselves into for a fee. Their latest client was a management company based in Miami. A company who represented a roster full of drug-addled celebrities who were always behaving badly.

"The clients live too far away, none of us are willing to move to Miami, so in my opinion we're not giving them a hundred percent effort. I think we can all agree that this isn't what we had in mind when Kat offered us the contract."

"But Miami is a huge chunk of our income."

"We were fine without it."

"Speak for yourself," Cutter says with a hard edge to

his words. "You have a rich daddy. The King brothers don't. We depend on every stream of income that comes in. You can't just unilaterally decide to turn off that stream. That isn't how a collaboration works!"

"I know how a fucking partnership works." Roman raises his thunderous voice about ten decibels. "And I'm going to need you to calm the fuck down, so that Elizabeth won't worry about what's going on in her house."

Roman and Cutter always verbally spar with each other while Camden sits back and allows them to hash it out. This is normal for them. It's just their way. Of course new brother doesn't know that yet and takes us all by surprise when he slams his hand down forcefully on the table.

Whack!

"I think everyone needs to calm the fuck down," Stone says, while staring menacingly at Roman. I'm going to be honest here, I've never seen someone outside of the Kings straight up challenge Roman before. In his own home at that.

Where's the buttered popcorn?

Where are my Raisinets?

This shit's going to be good. I think I'm feeling better already.

"Well look at who has a ball sack, Jade?" Roman says to me with an incredulous smile across his face. This is a smile I've seen before, and it's never a precursor to anything good. Egging Roman on probably wouldn't be smart right now, but I'm cranky today, so I just roll with it.

"I see that." I smirk.

“The fuck you say?” Stone challenges Roman again. I think I see a vein on the side of his temple popping out. Of course neither Cutter and Camden say anything to diffuse the situation. In fact, I catch the two of them smiling at each other across the table like they're two proud little brothers. I'm obviously the only one sitting in here with any sense.

"You should probably take a seat," I say to Stone. *Before Roman puts a fist in your jaw.* “Everything's fine. This is just how the boys talk to each other. You'll get used to it.”

Stone glares warily at everyone around the table then rests his eyes on Camden who's sitting with a satisfied look across his face. Cam quietly gives Stone a nod and motions for him to sit.

And he does.

I guess that's one of the things that I find so sexy about my guy. He doesn't even have to raise his voice to command the respect of the room, and as usual, he is the voice of reason.

"In typical Masterson family fashion, Roman, you've taken the room by surprise, but I know that you probably didn't come to this decision lightly. So Miami is dead. Fine. But Cutter is right. Do you have any plans for how to replace that income, because the Kings are splitting things three ways now?"

Stone shifts uncomfortably in his seat, and I can feel Roman looking at me from the side of his eye. I can already imagine what he's thinking. The same thing I am. Nobody told their asses to split their money three ways with a virtual stranger.

"Of course I do. I've already secured us a new client. They're local and they have a huge budget."

"Who is it?"

"The Provident Law Group."

CAMDEN

"She's not going to like this."

"She's not going to know."

"She ends up finding out everything."

I laugh a little at the exchange I'm having with Jade's sister Jana. I'm chatting with her through my car's Bluetooth system, while I'm on my way to meet my computer guy in the far Northeast section of the city. If I'm going to keep tabs on Provident, one of the largest law firms in Philadelphia, I'm going to need the help of someone who knows as much if not more, about computer systems as I do.

"I can keep a secret if you can."

"So how do you want to do this?"

"I want her to be speechless."

"Jade has pretty low expectations of men. I think that any grand gesture on your part will be well received."

"Thanks for that, Jana," I say sarcastically.

"Seriously though. Just pick out a pretty ring, and she'll say yes."

"I want to do better than picking out a pretty ring."

"Aww, you two make me want to believe in happily ever afters."

"What's up with that boss of yours?"

"You mean the professor?"

"Yeah."

"You think I'm interested in him romantically?"

"You talk about him a lot."

"Jade told you that didn't she?!"

"Nah, I'm just observant. You do realize that I'm in the same room with her when you speak to her half of the time."

"Remind me to tell her to switch rooms."

"Well stop calling her in the middle of the night then."

"You're always with her, so it doesn't really freakin' matter what time I call her now does it?!"

I chuckle to myself.

This girl is hysterical.

"Jana, the proposal. Are you going to help me plan it or not?"

"I'm not good at these types of things but if you insist."

"Then come up with some options as to how I can pull it off."

"Fine, but I still say you're overthinking this. Jade doesn't need to be bedazzled. The fact that she trusts you a hundred percent tells me everything I need to know. She'll say yes. She just wants you."

"And I just want her."

"Good, I guess we're in agreement then? No big gesture?"

She's not getting out of helping me.

"You've got until Thursday to come up with something."

"You're so bossy. The two of you are a match made in hell."

My stomach contracts with laughter, which is not the best thing, when you're driving on the notoriously dangerous Eastern Road.

"I thought just a minute ago we made you believe in happily ever afters."

"I retract my statement."

"You're a funny girl, Jana. I'll talk to you in a couple of days. In the meantime, make sure you don't get any bright ideas about sleeping with that professor, because then I'd have to hurt him or worse– ruin his credit report."

"You're diabolical."

"Agreed."

Click

"THIS MUST BE a big job you've got lined up."

"Yeah."

Samar is my go-to specialist when I need to double check a computer strategy that I might be considering for a fix. He's knowledgeable, trustworthy, and as far as I can tell a stand up guy, but I wouldn't say that we were friends. I don't have many of those. That's why I've never given him too many details about our fixes. Just enough to get the job completed.

"So you need to build and install an untraceable network that records all computer activity."

"Yep."

"How many computers?"

"Not sure. At least twenty-five. It's been a while since I've last been in there."

"All located in the same building, same floor?"

"Not all the time. I'm sure the laptops go home."

"So a mixture of desktops and laptops."

"Definitely."

"No problem. I have a couple of solutions to achieve that. It will be better though if you have direct access to their system."

"I will."

"They're hiring you?"

"Yes."

"Can you give me access as well?"

I pause for a moment. I've never brought Samar on a job with me (that would be muddying the waters), and I'm a little unclear as to why he's interested now.

"Why would I do that?"

"Would love to see you work. Plus it will be faster if we work as a team. What company hires one person to install or update a comprehensive computer network?"

"Samar, you're missing the point. They haven't hired me to update their network."

I'm not sure if Samar understands exactly what I do for people. I've told him that I'm a private contractor and nothing more. The less he knows about the sometimes illegal intricacies of what I do the better.

"So is that a no?"

"Let me think about it. I usually work alone. If it's money you need though, I can get you a little extra."

"Honestly, Mr. King, I need the distraction. My girlfriend went home to India to visit her sick mother, and now I'm having some trouble getting her back here."

"What kind of trouble?"

"Immigration trouble."

"Shit."

"Yeah, I should have never let her go home."

"Well it sounds like you didn't have much of a choice. How could you stop a daughter from going to see her sick mother. Family comes first."

Samar nods his head.

"Very true, Mr. King."

"So what kind of help do you need? Do you you need money?"

"I always need money. I have a huge extended family back in India that I help support, but I'm afraid money won't fix this. We just have to be patient and work our way patiently through the system. Hopefully I can get her back here for good."

"What's your citizenship status?"

I've never talked to Samar about personal shit before, and I'm starting to see why. Getting to know people actually forces you to give a damn, and giving a damn in our business can be a liability. I'm making an exception this time, but I probably shouldn't be.

"I was born in the U.S., so I'm fine, but I was visiting my family in India when I met Anika. I should have married her a long time ago, but I didn't want to rush things between us just because of her citizenship status. It wasn't like she was illegal or anything. She was here on a student visa. I just wanted us to date like normal. To see where things would lead without forcing anything."

Samar's head hangs low as he continues his story.

"Now I see how foolish I've been. Once she finished grad school, I should have married her. Now everything she's worked for is in jeopardy. She wanted a life here in the states with me not in India. She's going to have to work twice as hard to earn half as much there as she could here."

"Damn, you couldn't bring the mother here?"

"Her mother is dying. She wouldn't survive the trip. It was a risk, but Anika had to go there. It was bad timing. You're suppose to leave the U.S. sixty days after you graduate on a student visa. She'd been here four months. We knew it was a risk that they wouldn't let her come back. The plan was for her to get a job and apply for a work visa, but she still didn't have a full-time job yet when her mom fell ill. It's a tough market."

I must be getting softer, because after that story I actually consider hiring Samar to work with me on this job. Provident Law Group is a large company with a lot of employees and a huge network. There would be plenty for us both to do.

Nobody's going to like it, especially Roman, but that's the thing about me. I've never cared too much what people think.

Speak of the devil. It's Roman calling me on my cell.

"One second, Samar. I've got to take this."
"Hey, what's up? I'm in the middle of work."
"Come home now."
"What is it?"
"Jade collapsed."

ARIANA

I'm burrowing my head into the muscles of Stone's back as deeply as this fiberglass helmet stuck on my head will allow. We are riding a five-year-old Triumph Bonneville across the Pennsylvania Turnpike, pushing it way over the legal speed limit, or as Stone would say "airing the shit out".

I'd love to squeal with delight or even scream my head off in exhilaration like I've seen so many people do in the movies. Women who are riding on the back of some guy's bike with the wind blowing their hair back and laughing like they're having the time of their lives.

Not me though.

While I see why some people may like cruising the open road on a Harley (I've ridden on the back of my dad's bike many times), riding a sports bike is a completely different matter. The point of a Harley is to cruise. The point of this bike is speed. What started out as a good idea in theory, has turned into the ride from hell.

I'm petrified that we're going to crash into a guardrail and end up paralyzed.

My heart stops racing a mile a minute when we finally slow down, clearing the final tollbooth and veering onto a much slower local highway. We stop at a local mart, where we pick up a couple of food items before we head to our final picnic destination.

"I thought you were going to squeeze every vital organ out of my body back there." Stone chuckles quietly while he lays out the Native-American themed blanket we've brought along for our picnic.

"I think you left one of mine on the road a few miles back."

"Your father owns a bike shop."

"And your point?"

"I figured you were an experienced rider."

"I'm a nurse not a biker bitch."

My words seem caustic, because I don't get anything out of being frightened. I don't like horror movies, roller coasters, or jumping out of planes; and I damn sure don't like speeding across the highway on a bike.

"Told you I was airing it out today, babe."

I fluff out my helmet hair.

"I should have gone to work," I huff.

Stone slides one of his hands through my hair at the base of my scalp, pulling me into him, and kissing me softly on the side of my face.

"Take that back," he growls playfully in my ear.

"You never listen to me," I retort but I can feel myself faltering.

Stone's demanding growl sent an instant rush of moisture in between my legs.

"I thought I heard you giggling behind me on the bike."

"Those weren't giggles."

"They weren't?"

Stone takes a seat on the blanket and makes a patting gesture to sit next to him. I plop myself down and stretch completely out with my arms held high above my head.

"They were screams of terror."

He begins to kiss the side of my hips. Slowly sliding my t-shirt up. Not far though. Just enough so he can taste my skin.

"Well they both sound very similar. I thought you were having a good time back there."

"I'm sure the purple bruises that are going to show up on your ribcage tomorrow will prove my point."

He pops his head up. "Oh, I'm used to those," his words dripping with sexual innuendo. I do admit that I hold on a little tightly when Stone brings me to orgasm. It's possible that my nails may have inadvertently left a scar or two behind during our time together.

"Just pass me the bag of pretzels."

He taps my lips gently with his pointer finger as a signal to give him a kiss first. I willingly oblige. His lips are soft and lush. The complete opposite and compliment to the hard edges of his angular jaw.

He wraps one of his hands around my neck as he continues to explore my mouth with his tongue. Kissing me like it's the first and the last time. Making me desire more, but eventually pulling back.

"Now you can eat," he says playfully.

After I eat a handful of pretzels and swallow them down with a few swigs of bottled water, I lay face up on the blanket with my head resting on top of Stone's chest. The early afternoon sun warming my skin. Neither of us say anything for a moment, as we listen to the rise and fall of each others breaths.

Stone has mentioned many times how this was the type of the thing he missed most while in jail. Being free of the wall-to-wall concrete and simply enjoying the natural beauty of the outside world. That's why I've made it a point to find something for us to do outside, even if it's very small things like this, as often as possible.

He's the most laid back I've seen in weeks, so I decide it's a good idea to ask him about a subject which has been on my mind lately– work.

"So who's bike did we just air out?" I ask.

"Some new guy in the MC."

"What's his name?"

"Clint."

"Looks like you did a lot of work to it."

"I did. I'm hoping if he likes this one that he'll order a complete custom job."

"One that you build from the ground up?"

"Yeah–would love to do that shit."

I wring my hands together as I ask my next question.

"But wouldn't a project like that interfere in the work you're doing with Camden and Cutter?"

"They don't need me yet. I might be able to work both jobs for a while."

"But you don't need to. The Kings...they pay you a lot right?"

"I tried talking them out of it, but they won't listen. They say I'm blood, that I'm a King, and that they're not going to pay me a salary like some stranger."

"So why haven't you left the Riders?"

"I like working on bikes. Gotta keep busy until the brothers need me."

"So this new client of theirs, it's a law firm right?"

I need to be careful how I word this.

"Yep."

"So...what would you do for a law firm?"

Stone starts playing with my hair, winding my curls around one of his fingers.

"What do you mean, Ariana?"

"I'm just asking what you would be doing. They aren't just going to give you a third of their money for nothing."

"Are you worried about me?"

I'm not going to lie.

"Yes."

Stone slides one of his hands under my shirt at the collar and inside of my bra.

"Stone, we're outside," I half-heartedly protest.

"You worrying about me makes me want you even more than I already did."

He starts pinching one of my nipples until I start to squirm. First softly then hard. He continues alternating the pressure that he uses until I don't give damn that we're in a public park. Hell, it's a weekday. Kids should be in school.

"Have you ever had a fantasy about me making you come in a public place, Ariana? So loudly that people aren't sure if you are in need of assistance? So shrill that even the birds can hear you? So high that even God can hear you?"

"Stone."

My breath quickens.

"Answer me."

"No."

"But are you thinking about it right now?"

He moves to the other breast.

"Yes-s-s."

"If you're a really good girl we can make those fantasies come true in under five minutes, or if you're a bad girl I can draw this whole thing out for thirty."

"I want to be good. I want to come now," I say somewhat panting.

"Do you want bystanders to watch you come?"

"Ummm, no."

"Then wrap part of the blanket over top of you."

I follow Stone's instructions. My head still on his chest. His hand down my shirt. The bottom half of me covered by part of the blanket.

"Slide your hand inside of your jeans and touch yourself. Check if your wet."

"I already know–"

"I said to check."

I pause for a moment making sure that there's no one around. Even though we've selected a pretty secluded spot in the middle of a weekday, you never know. Anyone could be out here.

"Good girls don't hesitate, Ariana. Spread your legs."

"Stone!"

"You can keep the blanket on."

"I don't–"

Stone acts as if he can't hear a thing that I'm saying and slips his hand underneath the blanket. Working several of his thick fingers under the waistband of my jeans and inside my wet panties.

"You're soaked," Stone growls as he flicks my clit back and forth with two of his fingers.

I squirm harder.

"Put your hands under your shirt and take over for me. Play with your tits. No one can see you. You're with me. You're safe."

I don't care about anyone passing by at this point. My sex aches. My body is winding tighter and tighter. I want to come just as much as I want to breathe at this point.

Stone's fingers move with deft swiftness. Bringing my clit to life. Encouraging it to swell with desire.

"Stone!" My pleas come quicker now.

I beg for relief.

I beg for more.

I beg him to keep going.

I beg for him to stop.

I'm going to come very soon, and it's going be loud as hell.

"Come for me, Ariana."

My body contracts into a tight bow, and then I explode.

So loudly that I'm afraid even God hears.

STONE

I'm laying in bed, beside the woman who means everything to me, as I contemplate the fact that bad shit happens to people who get close to me.

I'm not wishing that on myself, but that's been my history. When Ariana asked me about what I'd be doing to earn my way as part of the King Brother trifecta yesterday, I couldn't answer her. I didn't want to.

The truth is that I'm probably going to be asked to do shit that I don't want anywhere near my girl. She's pure. Sweet. A nurse. A good daughter. Plus she's been through enough shit involving me.

What my brothers do for a living isn't for the faint of heart. They're paid to make bad shit go away or to make sure that it never happens. Unfortunately there's more jobs of the making problems go away variety than there is of the prevention jobs, which means they have to get their hands dirty a lot. As the business grows and they take on more elite clientele, not everyone can get their hands dirty. Which is where I come in.

Someone has to make the connections and solidify the fixes. That's Roman. Someone has to be the day to day voice of the company and run the fixes. I call him the show runner. That's Camden. Someone has to come in and negotiate when things run amuck. That used to be Cutter, but now that he's the primary manager of Club Lotus and the Tapas Lounge, he only comes in for certain cherry-picked cases. The rest of the negotiations are going to be my responsibility. In other words, I'm the one who's going to get my hands dirty the most.

Now don't get me wrong. I have no problem with keeping dirtballs in line. Especially if I'm getting paid for it. I'm just grateful that my brothers have accepted me into the fold like this. It's a huge deal that they are bringing a virtual stranger into the business. Into their lives. I plan on showing them that they didn't make a mistake in doing so. So if that means I need to knock a few heads together, I'll do it. Hell, I might even enjoy it.

The only problem I have is that this new job arrangement doesn't make Ariana happy. It makes her nervous. I'm on probation. If I slip up, I can easily get sent back to the clink.

My job repairing bikes for The Chosen Riders is a safe gig. She knows half of the men in the club. Her father knows the other half. She trusts them. If they are involved in any sort of illegal activity (which I imagine they are), it doesn't touch me. My partnership with my brothers though is a very different arrangement.

If I'm honest with myself, I know she's right. Taking on the job of negotiator and enforcer isn't the smartest thing to do in my situation, which is why I do my best to avoid discussing it with her. The less we talk about it the better. Talking is not my strong suit anyway.

I pull my head from between Ariana's legs to look at her. I'm checking to make sure her body's arched, her face is flush, and her pupils dilated. It's important that she's fully relaxed, before I move her on to other sorts of unchartered sexual territory. I am the man who took her virginity, and I take the responsibility of that shit seriously. I need to make sure that I'm careful with every new sexual experience I expose her to.

"Stone–" she pants.

"Yes, baby."

"Are you trying to sex me to death?"

I laugh.

"What do you mean?"

"I mean it's been three days straight of mind blowing sex, but I'm starting to think that it's some sort of stall tactic."

"Nah, baby. It's just good sex."

"Nothing with you is exactly as it appears."

"I promised you that I'd never to lie you again."

"I didn't say you were lying. You're stalling. Every time I ask you about working with your brothers, you commence with giving me an orgasm."

"Complaints?"

"Obviously I enjoy it but–"

"There's more where that came from. Now do you want me to finish what I started or not?"

"Stone."

"Shh, just tell me, what's your ultimate fantasy?"

"I want to talk about your new job."

She's not putting up with my crap today. Maybe I'm not putting in enough effort.

I lick closely around her clit. Blowing on it lightly. Making sure not to directly touch it with my tongue. Hoping this will drive her crazy. Crazy enough that she won't start asking for answers that I'm not ready to give her. My brother Camden asked me to come by his carriage house tonight. There is a lot going on, and they're ready to pull me in sooner than they anticipated.

My dick grows hard as a rock as Ariana's moans gain intensity. I want to love her. I want to protect her. I want to consume her.

"I need you, Stone."

"I know, baby. I need you too. Here I come."

I grab her hips, flip her over, and enter her swiftly. Usually I'm more careful when we fuck doggy style. Ariana always needs a moment to adjust to my girth when we do this position. It's her favorite so far, but I feel my lack of transparency with her about what I'm doing is creating distance between us. Distance I need to close. I guess that's why I'm claiming her body like my life depends on it.

Because it does.

"Ooh–" she coos almost reverently.

I close my eyes in bliss as I continue to stroke inside of her. Her body clenching and squeezing me like it never wants to let me go. If I was a crier, this would be the moment. That's how good it feels.

I slap her ass in approval and almost come when it jiggles.

"Fuck!" I roar.

I can't hold off too much longer. It's kind of embarrassing. I'm coming like a sixteen-year-old newbie who's whacking off to porn. I'm going to need to do better if I want to put off this conversation.

We both fall over in orgasmic bliss into the bed.

Panting.

Sweating.

Smiling.

"That was fantastic!" she says with a wide grin.

"Glad you approve, but I'm not finished. Come ride me, baby."

"Stone your phone has been buzzing nonstop."

"Leave it."

"It could be important."

It's obvious that she's not going to get on top of me until I check.

"Fine, give it here."

It's a text from Cutter.

Meeting location change.

Come to Penn Hospital cafeteria ASAP.

NEWS

NBA LEGEND FALLEN FROM GRACE

http://phillycelebmedia.com

LOCAL SPORTS LEGEND MURDER SUSPECT

An unidentified 20-year-old Massachusetts University college student was found dead in a Boston hotel room at approximately 2:45 this morning. According to sources, her partially nude body was found lifeless in the room of 52-year-old, legendary Philadelphia Basketball star and point guard, Dan Pearson.

Pearson was in Boston with five of his ball players from LaNova University where he is the head coach. The players were throwing a party in the hotel room where, according to sources, the woman was allegedly assaulted. Sources allege that the student, and one of the players ended up having a verbal dispute that turned violent when Pearson intervened. While Pearson is not in police custody at this time, sources tell us that he is a person of interest.

Pearson is married to former model Patricia Pearson and is the father of two daughters, Sloan and Dawn Pearson. None of whom could be reached for comment...and *gurl* can you blame them?

SLOAN

My sister is hysterical.

And I am...actually I don't know how I feel.

My father has pulled some shit in his day, but this is something on a whole other level. Even university administration is running from it. No one wants to touch this.

I'm coming home from a quick Starbucks run (caffeine is my drug of choice lately) when I notice my father's old Jaguar parked in front of my apartment.

He addresses me casually for a man in serious trouble.

"Hey, pumpkin."

My father practically has to unfold himself to get out of his car. I've always told him how his car is much too small for his six foot six body, but he loves that so-called collector's item too much to care about how it badly contorts his aging vertebrae.

"Hey, dad. This is a surprise."

"I guess you're wondering what brings me by."

Because you're a murder suspect perhaps?

"Do you want to come inside?" I offer.

My father hasn't visited me once since I've been with Cutter. There's something about him that rubs my dad the wrong way. He thinks I can "do better".

"I'd like that, Pumpkin. Thanks."

Once inside I raise some of the windows and check the cabinets for what I have on hand. I haven't eaten anything inside of my own apartment in at least three weeks. I'm always at Cutter's.

"Looks like I've got apple juice, Pepsi and diet cranapple juice. What's your preference?"

"I think I need something a little stiffer if you have it."

"Gotcha."

I fix my dad a gin and tonic, because I've been mixing my father's cocktails since I was twelve years old. I know exactly how he likes them. I pour my grande sized macchiato inside of a clean mug, and then I sit down across from him and wait.

We both know why he's here. What he wants to talk about, but I don't want to push things. My father and I have a very fragile rapport with each other. It's best if he leads this conversation.

My dad takes a long look around my place.

"Your set up is nice here, Sloan. You've done a lot since you first moved in. I'm impressed. You've got great taste like your mother."

"Thank you."

"Is your boyfriend around?"

"No, Cutter isn't here."

"Oh, okay." He takes a swig of his cocktail. "So it's

obvious why I'm here. I won't insult your intelligence with small talk."

"Appreciated."

Being Dan Pearson's daughter has never been easy. Being in this family has never been easy. It's always been a rollercoaster ride of his shenanigans and my family's emotional responses to them. I'm ready.

"The media has unnecessarily sensationalized this whole thing."

"A girl is dead, dad."

"Right, and I feel awful about that, but I swear to you I am innocent. All I wanted to do was help that girl."

I take a careful sip of my macchiato. It's still really hot.

"Why don't you start from the beginning."

"I took the boys on a trip."

My father is the head coach of the men's basketball team at a small city university located in Philadelphia–LaNova U. They are a division two team, so they rarely receive any national sports coverage, but the job is keeping him a part of the very thing that he loves more than life itself ... basketball.

"Got that part."

"It was just a small recruiting trip. There's a a kid in Boston who's a phenom, pumpkin. A beast. Maybe the next LeBron James." My father's face becomes animated with excitement. "He could change the whole trajectory of the program if we sign him."

Honestly, I don't care about this part of the story. A girl is dead.

"He's a high school senior, so you see I really had no choice. There are dozens of other programs that have been going hard at him for a long time now. He's going to make a decision soon. I had to put our bid in."

"Let me stop you here, dad. What does any of this have to do with what happened at the party?"

"I'm trying to explain to you why LaNova doesn't have my back. It isn't because I'm guilty or that they think I'm guilty of anything, it's because of the trip. It was outside of the NCAA sanctioned contact period for student athletes. We're actually only suppose to send letters and make phone calls during this time. I think they're punishing me."

Sometimes I wonder if my dad took a few too many hard elbows to the head during his days on the court. Why would he put his job in jeopardy like this? Now look at what's happened.

"Well, duh. I'm not surprised at LaNova's reaction then."

"Universities know about these trips, Sloan. They already knew I was going to Boston."

"So if the school thinks you're innocent and they knew about the trip, why don't they have your back?"

"No university is going to be caught green lighting a blatant violation of NCAA rules."

“Especially now that the whole trip is attached to a murder."

"Even worse."

"Have they talked about suspending you?"

"Worse."

"Fired?"

My father needs his job. He's still too young to start collecting his pension, and he's too old to play ball. He's left with either coaching or commentating, and no network has shown any interest in giving him a permanent spot, and after this they never will.

"My employment is under review."

Good grief.

"So continue telling me what happened."

"The boys wanted to throw a party at the hotel. They wanted to show the recruit a good time. Show him how much of a family we are, and how much fun it can be to be on the team.

"They consumed quite a bit of beer and liquor that night, and things got out of hand midway through the party. Obviously there were girls there, but there was this one girl in particular, a student from Boston U. Some hanger on. A party girl. She came to me, drunk, and accused one of the boys of hurting her."

"You mean raping her?"

"Yes," he agrees a bit too dismissively for my taste. "And the girl was hysterical. Yelling, knocking stuff over. I was trying to calm her down."

I sit silently for a moment and take a few deep breaths. I love my father to death, but I think he has always been a boy cloaked in a grown man's body. He's never truly embraced the responsibilities of a husband and a father. I can see why he always hired security back in the old days. He needed babysitters, because he makes such poor choices.

"Why were you at the party?"

My father hangs his head.

"It was a poor decision."

Exactly.

SLOAN

I take another deep cleansing breath.

"Were you partying with those kids, dad?"

"Some of them were being too noisy in the hallway. I had to get them inside of the room before someone complained and I stayed. I figured I'd keep an eye on things. Plus, I guess I was a little bored in my room by myself."

Stupid.

"So go on. What happened after she made the accusations?"

"Like I said, she was screaming. Making a scene. I asked her numerous times to calm down. She said she couldn't. That she'd just been attacked and she wanted to know what I was going to do about it."

"Who did it?"

"She said it was Bobby Thornton, Tommy Newton and Chris Speedwell."

"A gang bang?!"

"Yes."

"And did you believe her?"

My father rubs his jaw sternly.

"Being a collegiate athlete comes with it's pros and cons. There's a lot of pressure put on you to perform, to win, to keep up your grades, to never make a mistake. It's a really heavy load for a young man."

I've heard this speech my entire life.

Over it.

"Dad, let me cut you off there. I don't care if that girl was drunk and rubbing her naked hoohah in that guy's face. That doesn't ever excuse having sex with a woman without her consent."

"That's not what I'm saying, Sloan."

"Then what are you saying?"

"I'm saying that sometimes the lines get muddled. Those boys get a yes so much and so often, that sometimes they think they've got a green light to go ahead when they really don't. Especially when you mix it with drugs and alcohol."

"They thought they had a green light to a gang bang?"

"A lot of these girls do consent to group sex."

"In porno movies maybe, but please continue with your story."

My father lets out an exasperated sigh.

"The boys started getting loud with her when they noticed what she was saying to me. There was name calling and raised voices. A few threats. It was getting out of hand and that's probably when I should have called for some help, but I didn't. I didn't want anyone finding out about the party, the attack, or the fact that I was there.

"Anyway, the girl and her friend felt like they were being ganged up on. They were scared. There were all these six and seven foot tall ball players, drunk, yelling at her. Threatening her. So her and her girlfriend started swinging. Like they were cornered animals. Teeth snarling and everything.

"It all happened so fast. I remember having my hands up in a defensive pose. Trying to calm her and the boys down at the same time, but somehow in the melee, she got hit. She fell and hit her head on the corner of the coffee table and that was it. I saw the light go out of her eyes instantly. I knew immediately that she was gone."

I am quiet for a moment. Thinking about that girl's last hour on earth. How frightened she must have been. How sad. Thinking about the many times my father had a chance to make a different decision.

"You don't know who hit her?"

"No one is stepping up and saying that they did it."

"Yes, but do you *know* who hit her."

"No, there were too many people. I can't say for sure."

I shake my head in disgust. Only my father would find himself in such a fucked up situation.

"I don't know what to say, dad."

"I just thought I should let you know the truth of what's going on. I haven't been brought in on any formal charges yet, but things aren't looking good. That girl's family is looking for blood...and money. So you know, just be careful about what you post on social media and all that for a while. Keep a low profile."

My father finishes the last swig of his drink and slowly gets up. Grimacing a little as he rises on his arthritic knees and a battle worn lower back. All in all, my father is pretty calm, and saying all the right things, but I can tell that he's stressed and that there may be something else he isn't saying.

"Is there anything else?"

"I just...well I think my lawyer may need some help."

"What kind of help?"

“Like finding out who actually is responsible may be my only chance. It's hard though. I don't just want to go around asking my kids to rat on each other."

"This is your life though.”

"I know. It's just...maybe someone else should do the asking."

"Yeah, like the police or your lawyer."

"Listen I know that you are in the middle of planning your wedding, and that I haven't been the most supportive father of your relationship, but I need Cutter's help. Without it I think the police have already made their decision on who the murderer is. Me."

Shit.

"I know this is a big ask, but I'm desperate, Sloan."

I'm conflicted. I don't want my father to go to jail, but I also don't want to ask Cutter to do this. I've been reluctant to make a commitment to the apartment, to the wedding date, but then I ask him to take my father on as a fix? Not cool. Not fair.

"I'll let you know, dad."

My father startles me by kissing me on the cheek. Something he hasn't done probably since the day I graduated from college.

"Thank you, pumpkin."

That's how I know, that he's desperate. I at least have to ask.

SLOAN

Cutter looks just like a little boy when he sleeps. An angelic boy. His limbs are full extended but relaxed at the same time. I watch as his chest rises and falls quietly. Counting his breaths. It's at moments like these that I know for sure that I love this man, because if he ever stopped breathing, I would want to stop breathing too.

The visit from my father put a lot of things in perspective. My reluctance to commit has clearly stemmed from the fact that I've had a lifelong reluctance to trust. Especially trusting men. I used to think that men were only good for some things. To look at. To sleep with. To fix things around the house. But to share a life with? Hell, no.

Even though I've been going through the motions of being in a relationship, up until this moment, I've always had one foot in and one foot out the door. It's only now that I understand why Elizabeth has been pushing me with both hands into this wedding. I needed the push, and I didn't even realize it or why. Now I do.

I'm not being fair to my man or to myself. Unlike my father, I have to commit. That's why today I've made two decisions for the sake of our relationship.

1. We're going to set a wedding date.

2. I'm not going to ask him to help my father.

The weather has been growing a bit more humid lately, so last night Cutter and I slept with the windows up under a light cover and in the nude. I lift the cover to take a peek. What a magnificent man. My man.

Even though he's sound asleep, it's just too tempting, so I slide my hand under the sheet and begin to slowly bring Cutter's cock to life.

"Good morning to you too," he says with his eyes still closed and a smile on his face.

"Good morning, lover."

"What did I do to deserve this delightful morning greeting?"

"Exist."

All of a sudden Cutter roughly rips the cover off of us. Sending it sailing through the air and onto the floor. He yanks me up and pulls me on top of him.

"You're saying all the right shit this morning. Ride my face. Now!" he growls.

My palms slap against the wall behind the bed as Cutter works my pussy in the most delicious way. The sensations of his warm morning mouth all over my sex are almost unbearable in the best way.

"Cutter," I moan from deep within.

He lightly slaps each of my butt cheeks as I continue to writhe in agony and grind my pelvis against his face.

"That's a good girl," he praises. The vibrations of his

words bouncing against my skin and every one of my clitoral nerve endings. "Work that pussy for me, Princess."

Something indiscernible leaves my mouth.

Something primal.

Something dominant.

I flip myself around. Still allowing him to eat me out, but positioning me to pleasure him as well. The perfect sixty-nine position, and it looks like it was a good decision. His dick is practically weeping.

I hear guttural noises coming from deep in Cutter's chest as I work my mouth up and down his shaft. He's going to come quickly. Maybe even before I do. I almost feel like it's a race. To see who can finish first or rather who can last the longest.

"You ready to come?" he says into my skin.

"Are you?" I respond with a mouth full of him.

"Keep sassing me, and I'm getting the rope."

"Get it," I challenge.

"HEY, I just got a text. Something's up with the little hobbit. I'm going to need to head over to Penn Hospital in a few," Cutter says as we lay post coital in the bed.

"Is Jade ok?"

"The text didn't sound like he was about to choke anyone, so it can't be all that bad. We're probably just going to have the meeting at the hospital instead of the restaurant. He's definitely not going to set one foot outside of the hospital until that woman is back in tip top condition."

True.

"You want eggs or a bagel with your bacon?"

"Eggs and make my bacon crispy."

"Okay, bossy, I know how you like your bacon."

"I know you do, but I'm just making sure."

"Stop topping from the bottom, Sloan."

"What are you my master now?"

"In all things and in every way. Don't ever forget it, darlin'."

I laugh although he's definitely right about one thing. Cutter King is the master of my body. He literally made me feel like I was floating outside of it this morning. I should try taking charge in bed more often. It drives him nuts. He always has to "punish" me afterwards, yet somehow it always feels like a reward.

"So I'd like to us to set an August date."

Cutter lays the last slice of bacon in the frying pan then turns towards me in disbelief.

"August?"

"For the wedding," I say casually.

"To me?"

"Cutter."

"Is this about your father? You think he's going to jail, so you're in a hurry to get down the aisle?"

"What? No."

"You haven't brought up his situation to me since you found out about it. That tells me something, Sloan. You're not dealing with it well. You're pretending like it's all going to magically work out. Like your not worried when I know that you have to be."

"There's nothing to talk about. My father has a gang of

well paid lawyers and the truth on his side. He'll get himself out of this mess. I'm sure this won't even be an issue in another week or so."

"You're sure that you're ok?"

"Me wanting to get married in August has nothing to do with his case and everything to do with the fact that I just pulled my head out of my ass."

"Do tell."

"I'm engaged to the only man on this earth who I trust with my life. A man who never makes a stupid decision (well at least most of the time). The one man who has my back. The only man I love or will ever love. "

I stand on my tiptoes and wrap my arms around his neck.

"Marry me, Cutter."

He bends over. Hanging his head low by my ear.

"In August?" he whispers.

"Whenever you want, my liege." I rub my hands over his freshly shorn head. A sound emits from his chest similar to the purring of a cat. "Just tell me when and where, and I'll be there."

"Then August it is, Mrs. King."

He kisses me passionately as our breakfast bacon burns to a crisp.

"And move all of your shit out of your apartment and in here by the end of the week."

I giggle to myself.

"Yes, sir."

CAMDEN

"Sit down. You're hovering and it's making me nervous."

"Ditto."

"What do you mean ditto?"

"You're making me fucking nervous too."

"I fainted, Cam. People faint everyday. You've got to relax. You're just in a pissy mood that you can't control this situation like you do everything else."

"Fainting is not normal. You shouldn't have gone to work. I shouldn't have let you go to work. You've been sick for days. Roman knew that shit. I should–"

"Roman is not at fault. I think I was simply overheated. It was hot in his house. Something about the compressor on the central air unit needing to be replaced."

"Jade...is it possible that you're pregnant?"

"What exactly are you accusing me of?"

"Did that sound like a fucking accusation? I'm just asking you if you're pregnant. In the family way. With child. Did I knock you up?!"

"Absolutely not."

"You seem shocked that I'm even asking about the possibility."

"I am a little."

"Why? We have sex– repeatedly."

"I also take the pill– daily."

"The pill isn't foolproof, but let's table this discussion for now. I don't want you to get *overheated* again."

"Funny."

Some doctor with a fucked up last name, Jeremy Dick MD, comes in the room with another man and woman following closely behind him. Both in scrubs and white coats.

Penn is a teaching hospital, so it's to be expected that there will be more than one person in the room, but I don't like it. I asked for a department head, not an attending physician and his flunkies.

Dr. Dick glances at his clipboard in a very perfunctory way and then looks at Jade over top of his reading glasses.

"Miss Barlow."

"Yes."

"Heard you had a fall today."

"Yes."

"How are you feeling now?"

"A little weird but not as badly as before. I think I'm just dehydrated or something."

"Stop trying to diagnose yourself, Meredith Grey, and let the doctor here do his job," I say in a sarcastic voice.

The two residents try suppressing a few giggles at what I've said, but Doctor Dick ignores me as if I'm not even in the room and continues with his questions. Yeah, I definitely don't like this dude.

"Do you work out, Miss Barlow?"

"Yes."

"What do you do?"

"Running. Weights. Spin. Sometimes pilates."

"Did you work out today?"

"No."

"She hasn't been feeling well for days," I interject.

Again, he ignores me.

"Have you been taking your pill regularly?"

"Yes."

"Have you ever had any problems with the pill or any other kind of birth control?"

"No."

The doctor makes some notes, flips through some of the papers on his clipboard for a moment, and then speaks again.

"I'd like to talk about your family history a little now."

"Okay."

"Are both of your parents living?"

"No. My mother is deceased and my father...well he's actually dying."

"Of what?"

Put some sympathy in your voice, Dr. Dickhead.

"Cancer."

"What kind?"

"I don't know exactly."

"And your mother. What was the cause of death?"

Jade pauses for a moment. Swallowing hard. It's hard for her to talk about her mother. Sometimes I forget that

Cutter and I got to have a bit longer with our mother than she did with hers. So we have memories. Jade doesn't have many good ones. All she remembers is her mother being sick.

"Ovarian cancer."

Dr. Dick gives Jade a look that chills me to the bone.

"Do you get regular pap smears, Miss Barlow?"

"Yes."

"Have they ever come back irregular?"

"No."

He glances at me for the first time, then my tattoos, and then back at Jade.

"Any venereal diseases?"

She clears her throat. "No."

I'm ten seconds away from choking him with that fucking stethoscope.

"Okay, well I think we're going to need to do a little more testing. Dr. Keller here is going to take your blood pressure and the nurse will be in here shortly to take some more blood and run an IV. Then we're going to send you up to gynecology. I'd like to get another pap smear."

Oh, shit.

Does he think she has cancer?

Jade turns her face to me, and I see the fear in my heart reflected back in her widening pupils. I cradle the side of her face with my hand and wipe the one lone tear running down her face with my thumb.

"It's going to be fine, baby."

She nods her head, but I can tell she's terrified.

"I'm ruling things out, Miss Barlow," the jackass says. "There are a ton of medical reasons why you could have fainted today. None of them serious, but it doesn't hurt to rule everything out."

"How long are these additional tests going to take?" I ask.

"The nurse should be in shortly. Gyno may take another thirty minutes. Then we have to wait for the results. So expect to be here for most of the day."

I hate hospitals.

"Don't call Jana," Jade asks while the male intern gets the blood pressure cuff ready. "She'll freak, and we don't know if there's anything to freak out about yet."

In my panic, I called everyone, but there's no way I'm going to let Jade know that. I can hold Jana off.

"No problem. I've got you."

She nods her head with relief.

"Thank you."

Jade is sitting on the edge of the examination table. Her hands gripping the edge of it. Her legs dangling off of the side. She looks more vulnerable than I've ever seen before.

I want to wrap myself around her and protect her from the world right now. My tough girl holds it together for all of us all of the time when inside I know she's soft as butter.

"No thank you's are necessary between us, baby."

I lean down and press my mouth onto hers. Saying a silent prayer to myself, to God, or to whoever will listen as I do.

Please let her be all right.

Please don't take her from me.

"Listen, I'm going to step out while they take your

pressure and all of that. I'll be right back." I give the two interns a stern look. "Unless you don't want me to leave."

"Go ahead," Jade chuckles while squeezing my hand. "I'm fine."

"Okay, baby. I'll be back in thirty. I love you."

"Ditto." She smiles.

CAMDEN

My brothers and I were supposed to meet later tonight at the tapas lounge about the Provident job, but I'm meeting with them in the hospital cafeteria instead. That's the great thing about family. At least this family. They always have your back.

"How is she?" Cutter asks with concern etched in his face.

"We don't know much yet. They're still running tests."

"Stone's not here yet?"

"No, he's on his way."

"So she passed out at Roman's?"

"Yeah– Roman said she was fine when he went to give Elizabeth her lunch, but when he got back to the room Jade was on the floor unconscious."

"Shit that's scary."

"Yeah."

"And uh, Roman makes lunch?"

I crack a smile at that.

"I guess he does. So listen, I wanted to talk to you

about something real quickly before Stone gets here. He's about five minutes away."

"What?"

"Our first client out of Provident is a ball player."

"Sweet. Who is it? Anyone I know?"

"Not a professional. It's a kid. Plays for LaHova. Name is Tommy Newton."

Cutter's face drops.

"Please tell me that he has nothing to do with that party and Sloan's father," he says.

"I'm afraid that is has everything to do with him."

"What's a Division Two kid like that doing with Provident's level of legal representation?"

"He's not being represented by the talent division but rather the criminal division."

"So he probably killed the girl."

"Yeah, that's what I'm thinking."

"Why else would he hire a firm so high-powered?"

"Samar got access to a few conversations they had. Not much. But what he did hear disturbed me. The kid has a few NBA teams interested in signing him which explains why Provident is involved. It seems as if the kid and his lawyer are trying to build a defense naming Dan Pearson as the one who hit the girl, and getting as many people as they can to support his statement. He may have already got four kids to roll on Pearson already."

"Fuck me."

"What has the glamazon said about it?"

"She talked to her father and is convinced that he has it all under control. That he has the truth on his side."

"So she's delusional."

“Pretty much. So who's the kid's lawyer?"

"That's the only good thing. It's Prentis. You remember him from a couple of years back right? At least we know him. We can get to him.“

"Fuck!"

"What?"

“‘Lazy eye’ Prentis is in the middle of hiring Sloan for a design job, and there's no way that shit is a coincidence. He’s probably pumping her for information as we speak, and she can’t even see it coming.”

"That asshole. He's got some balls on him."

"I want to put that kid Newton and Prentis under the fucking jail."

"Noted– but since murder is not on the menu, let's think of an alternate plan."

"Sloan finally set a date. I'm getting married in three months. The guy is probably not ever going to be father-in-law of the year, in fact, he won’t even acknowledge my existence, but I can’t allow him to be convicted, Cam. In fact he can never go to trial. It will kill Sloan. That kid has to confess and do it quickly."

"Married in fucking August, eh?” I slap my brother on the shoulder. "Congratulations, little brother. Let's fix this shit then."

Looking just like our missing triplet, our brother Stone finally enters the cafeteria. He glances at the both of us then takes a seat.

"What did I miss?”

"You've been assigned your first fix, big brother," I say. "His name is Tommy Newton. He's twenty years old. Ball player at LaNova. And we need him to sing like a bird."

“Is that all? Done."

Cutter smiles with relief.

"How's wifey?" Stone asks me.

Wifey. I know it's just a term some men use to describe a long term girlfriend, but it gets me really thinking. Jade should be my wife. My legal wife. She's it for me. And if she's sick, I'm going to hold her hand through every step as her husband. Not just some dude she's fucking.

"She's going to be good, man. I'll make sure of it."

JADE

There is nothing fun about hospitals. They're sterile and cold and you can't get a good blanket to save your life.

My mother died in a hospital. I don't remember everything about that day. I just remember thinking that my mom must have been cold, and that she probably wanted her fluffy white blanket with the small pink roses on it.

I want out of here.

When the doctor returns to my room it's sooner than I anticipated. The IV must be kicking in because my stomach feels more settled. That's why I sent Camden out to buy me a green drink from somewhere. I'm hungry.

"How are you feeling, Miss Barlow?"

"Pretty good."

Several men roll another bed in next to me.

"What's this?" I ask looking between it and the doctor.

"Where's your boyfriend, Miss Barlow?"

"He stepped out. Why?"

"We discovered what the issue is and we're taking you in for emergency surgery. Can you sign the consent please?"

I need Cam.

"Consent for what?!"

"Your hCG levels were abnormally high. Upon further examination we discovered the issue. You are pregnant and it's ectopic. Meaning the baby is growing in your fallopian tube. We need to operate now. Your life is at risk."

"I need to call my boyfriend."

I feel like I'm about to hyperventilate.

"Sign the consent and this privacy form which will allow us to share your medical information with him, and we will make sure to tell him everything he needs to know when he gets back."

I quickly sign the papers, not exactly sure what I'm signing, but petrified that if I don't– I will die right here in this room. Alone. Unable to say goodbye to the man I love.

"Here."

"Gynecology knows what they're doing at this hospital, Miss Barlow. They're top 20 in the country. You're in good hands. Dr. Medwick will be performing your surgery and will be here shortly to brief you and start your procedure ok?"

"Yes."

Tears start to roll down my face.

"Can I text my boyfriend now?"

"You really shouldn't because of all of the sensitive

medical equipment in this room but go ahead. One quick text. I'm sure you want him here."

I can't do this without him.

"Thanks."

Me: They have to operate:(Come back now.

STONE

"What are you doing?"

Because I am a felon, I'm not licensed to carry, but that doesn't mean I can't toss a few baseball bats in the back of my Chevy truck.

"Have to work," I explain to Ariana.

"What are you a Little League coach now?"

"Protecting myself."

"From who?"

"Are you sure you want to know?"

I will never lie to Ariana again, although sometimes it's a difficult promise to keep. I never want to see the look she has on her face right now. All I want to see are smiles and laughter and of course...pleasure.

"Yes."

"A killer."

"What?! Does this have something to do with your brothers?"

"Yes, but it involves your friend too."

"Which friend?"

"Sloan."

"What about her?"

"One of the kids that plays for her father at LaNova is setting him up for that girl's murder charge."

"Setting him up?"

"Yes, and I need to stop it."

"You?"

"Why not me?"

"You know why. You don't need to put yourself in harm's way, Stone."

"Cutter needs me."

"For what? Why can't he handle it? He'd do anything for Sloan. He's in love with her."

"Exactly. He's too close to this. He might end up accidentally killing the kid if the guy says the wrong thing. I'm a lot more detached. It's a job to me. Nothing more."

"I don't like it."

"I get that."

"But it doesn't matter to you?"

"You matter to me, but my brothers matter too. I want to work with them, Ariana. This is how I'll get to know them. This is how we can start to make up for all of the time we missed. Nothing's going to happen to me. You worry too much."

I wrap my hand around her waist and pull her into me.

"Give me my kiss," I say.

I slide my hand into the back of her hair and give her a firm kiss on the mouth. I love this mouth.

"You trust me right?"

"Yes, of course. It's just that I worry."

"I know and I love that you do. Nobody's ever given a

shit about me but my dad and you, but I'm a lot more convincing than you give me credit for. This kid will back down in less than ten minutes. No muss. No fuss. I guarantee it."

She turns her lips up to one side in disbelief, but I continue talking.

"And Ariana– we can't have this discussion every time I go to a fix. This is what I do now. You're either going to roll with it or you're not. I rather you roll with it."

"Stone–"

I lean over and swiftly lift her up by her butt and hips. Instinctively she wraps her arms around my neck and her legs around my waist.

"Roll with it," I growl into her neck.

She sighs softly.

It's working.

"Roll with it," I say again as I my dick hardens.

"I'm rolling with it," she says quietly as she kisses the side of my ear.

Her body softens in my grasp.

"Fuck, Ariana, I have to go to work."

"I know, I know. You have to go scare a kid to death. But how about you bang me silly on this bed before you go."

My body grows taut.

I love it when my angel talks dirty.

"Bang you?"

"Fuck me."

Jesus.

"You've got fifteen minutes. Where do you want me?"

"I only need ten, and I want to ride you."

Fuck me, I love this woman.

"You drive a hard bargain."

Then I toss her ass on the bed as she squeals with delight and get to making love to my woman.

THIS IS EASIER than I thought it would be. I'm used to keeping hardened killers at bay in prison, so I put my strongest emotional battle armor on when I went to find Tommy Newton. Ready to scare the fuck out of him. Ready to strip him of his humanity.

But this is the real world, not prison, and Tommy Newton is just some entitled basketball playing kid from the suburbs who doesn't want to pay the consequences for his bad decisions. Making him see the light is easy work. If this is all I have to do for a living everyday, then I'm going to be a fucking millionaire.

"Mindy Newton. Oliver Newton. Kara Newton. Laura Newton."

I've cornered Newton outside of the Plymouth Meeting Mall. He just finished having dinner with some unsuspecting girl. Didn't even have the decency to walk her to her car after they were finished. Just patted her on the ass and sent her on her way.

"Who arrrre you, dude?" he stutters a bit while staring at what I'm holding in my hands. "Why are you naming everyone in my family?"

"Because that's who I'm going to visit one by one with each of these fucking baseball bats if you don't take responsibility for what you did in Boston."

"I didn't do nothin'."

"You sucker punched that girl *after* you raped her and now you're letting your coach take the fall. You're a real prick you know that?"

"I didn't do it!"

I lift up one of the lighter bats. The black and grey aluminum one.

"Say you didn't do it again, and Mindy is first."

I wouldn't actually hit Mindy Newton with a baseball bat. I think the woman is his grandmother and is probably eighty years old, but he doesn't know that. I'm sure he looks at my height, my ink, my scars and thinks that I would do exactly what I say. At least that's what I'm counting on.

"Coach Pearson was there. I mean...he was yelling at her too."

I swing the bat towards Tommy's head but stop it in mid-air. He flinches and covers his head with his hands like I knew he would.

"Pussy." I laugh. "Say that shit again, and I will visit Oliver next. He works at the mini mart around the corner from your house right?"

"Wait–"

"I'm listening."

"I'll go tell my lawyer that I'm recanting my statement, but you have to promise to leave my family alone."

"No need to waste his time. You'll go straight to the station and confess."

"I need a lawyer first!"

"After your confession. And let me warn you right

now, this isn't a negotiation. This is a ultimatum. You feel me?"

He hesitates for a moment. So I lift all of my bats and rest them on my shoulders, staring at him square in his eyes.

"I'll go right now," he acquiesces.

"Right answer, homie. I'll follow you to the station."

SLOAN

"So how are you holding up?" I ask my mother.

I've talked to my sister Dawn at least three times a day since the news broke about my father, but have yet to speak to my mother about it. She doesn't like to talk on the phone. She's more of a "let's meet and have drinks" type of person. So we're here together meeting at a local restaurant near her yoga studio.

"As good as can be expected. Some of those yoga hussies are talking about me behind my back in class, but I'm ok."

"Namaste, bitches." I say while bowing my head and motioning the prayer sign with my hands.

My mother cracks a smile.

"So how did you find out?" she asks.

"He came by the apartment."

"Oh, so he finally visited you in your love shack?"

"He doesn't know that Cutter bought the building yet. Not unless you told him?"

"I didn't."

"I figured as much."

"So what did he want? He came all the way over there to tell you about the incident?"

"He wants Cutter's help."

"Of course. Typical Dan. He wants help from the same man he won't even acknowledge."

My mother pauses to pop a few mystery pills into her mouth and washes them down with some ice water.

"I know, but I guess desperate times called for desperate measures."

"So is Cutter the one who got him off then?"

"What?"

"Didn't you hear? Your dad is no longer a person of interest. The police told us last night and the news broke just this morning."

"How? I mean I know he has a great group of lawyers, but this seems almost like a miracle. It was looking bad there for a while."

"It wasn't anything the lawyers did. The kid confessed on his own."

"Which kid?"

"Tommy Newton. Even though he's pleading not guilty to rape and murder, he did admit to hitting that poor girl in self-defense. His confession simply proves that he's a liar. So it's just a matter of time before they build a rock solid case against him."

"Wow."

"I know– I can't believe that I had that little rapist over to my house for spaghetti dinner."

"You cook now?"

"Uber Eats."

"Oh...well this is great news, but you seem kind of callous about the whole thing. I mean dad was in serious trouble for a minute there. He may never shake the stigma of being a murder suspect. His reputation is ruined."

"Reputation?" she scoffs. "Well there's a part of the story that I'm sure he conveniently left out when he came running to you for help."

"What else?"

"There was another girl at the party. The friend of the dead girl. Your father was seeing her."

"What do you mean *seeing*?"

"Exactly what you think I mean. Evidently she's someone he's been "visiting" when he travels to Boston. He's been there at least four times over the last three months. Supposedly she was at that party with your father. To see your father. I guess they were *busy* in another room which is how her friend ended up drunk and alone and getting raped by some of the players. From what I've been told, the victim, I mean that poor girl, accused your father of setting her up. That's why she confronted him."

Oh my God.

"She thought dad set her up to get assaulted? That's crazy."

"People start to think irrationally when alcohol is involved."

"And how do you know all of this again?"

"Your father told me."

"He told you all of this? About the girl and everything?"

"He tells me mostly everything after the fact, and I

don't expect you to understand why he does or why I listen or why I stay, but you will one day when you're married."

I hope I never understand this type of twisted dysfunction.

My parents were in love once. I know because I'm pretty sure I saw glimpses of it as a little girl, but mostly because their courtship was documented ad nauseum in many of the celebrity magazines back in the day. But based on my father's long time bad behavior, I'm not sure what their marriage has become now.

At this point I guess it's a marriage of convenience, because there is no other explanation for why a woman as beautiful and intelligent as my mother would continue to put up with my dad's chronic womanizing.

My marriage is going to be a lot different. That I'm sure of.

"I'm sorry, mom. I really am."

"Nothing new right? He's going through some sort of mid-life crisis, and he isn't seeing things straight. He thinks this girl, this child, might be his soulmate. He wants to see her through this. Be there for her as she mourns for her friend. Never mind what his family may want or need. Never mind the bad publicity and the whispers I get behind my back."

"You should leave, mom."

"And give some twenty year old bitch my life?"

I didn't think so.

"Mom, I'm getting married in August.

"This August?"

"Yes."

"Is marriage what you really want?"

"It is."

"Even after everything I've just told you?"

"Cutter is nothing like daddy. He is everything a husband should be."

"You're not dazzled by the dick are you?"

"Mom!"

"I've seen Cutter without a shirt and basketball shorts on. He is definitely something to look at. But make smarter choices than me, Sloan."

"Trust me I am."

"You might be right, because I don't know why that Newton boy would confess unless he had a really good reason to. I'm thinking your fiance had something to do with it."

"Cutter? Uh-uh."

"Why not? He loves you and helping people in trouble is what he does for a living."

"I didn't want him involved in our family mess, so I never asked him for his help. In fact, I haven't really said much about dad's whole case to him. I wanted distance from it, and dad has always been able to weasel out of trouble by throwing money at it."

"You know, Sloan, even though your father is an immature jerk most of the time, he loves his family. He always has."

I give my mother a look like she just grew three horns out of her head. My father can do almost anything to her, to us, to himself, and she'll still find a way to defend him.

"Uh, I guess, but he loves himself more."

The server places our drinks down and my mother takes a sip of her iced tea as if it were a shot of vodka.

"I know I seem like a rock to you, Sloan. Emotionless. Steady. Unbothered. But I'm not. I've been with your father from the very beginning. When he was in college and blew out his knee, there were no guarantees that he would have a pro career, but it didn't matter to me. I would have stayed either way. I loved him. But he's betrayed me so many times that I've lost count, and all that I have left is you and my philanthropy work."

“So why are you defending him?”

“I'm not. I just don't want you going through life thinking that your father doesn't give a damn about you. He loves you, he's proud of you, and in my opinion he's been a pretty good father. He's just a terrible husband.”

My mother begins eating her meal in the methodical way that she always has since I was little. Protein first, veggies second, a small forkful of her starch third, and then a sip of unsweetened iced tea with lemon to wash it all down.

She's absolutely miserable. I wish for once that she could be happy. Genuinely happy.

Like I am.

"Do you think dad will leave you for this girl?"

"Leave me?" she scoffs. "He was never going to leave. He's just planning to set up house with her. Sleep at home during the week and sleep wherever he sets up house for her on the weekends. He's with her right now. In Boston. As soon as the police gave him the all clear, he was on the first thing smokin' out of Philadelphia.“

I almost spit out my mouth full of Shirley Temple,

which I ordered as a joke, because I couldn't wait to see my mother's face when I tied the stem of the cherry into a knot with just my tongue.

"You can't be serious."

"That's what he said."

I place my fork full of fish down, and cross my arms on the table top.

"He's not invited to my wedding!"

My mother grins.

"Sloan...don't be so dramatic."

Me: Did you have something to do with getting my dad off the hook?

Cutter: Where are you?

Me: In an Uber. Answer the question.

Cutter: Why are you asking me that?

Me: Just. Answer. The. Question.

Cutter: Maybe.

Me: I didn't ask you to do that.

Cutter: You didn't have to.

Me: What did you do?

Cutter: It wasn't actually me. I knew about it of course, but it was all Stone, and he was glad to do it.

Me: Really? Stone did it?

Cutter: Yep.

Me: So I guess I have to be nicer to him now?

Cutter: That would be great, yes.

Me: But I rather be really nice to you when I get home in about fifteen minutes.

Cutter: How nice?

Me: Roll your eyes in the back of your head nice. On my knees nice. Arms tied behind my back nice.

Cutter: Get the fuck home NOW!

Me: I'm cummmin...sir.

CAMDEN

It seems as if every time Jade needs me, I'm no where to be found. I've spent every waking moment in the hospital, yet the moment I go on a store run for her, she's rolled into emergency surgery.

I ran six city blocks in record time after getting her text. Green juice flying everywhere. My heart beating furiously through my chest. What if she's frightened? What if the surgeon doesn't know what he's doing? Why is it an emergency? Is she dying?

When I ran to the floor she was on and saw Doctor Dickhead casually talking on his cell phone at the nurse's desk, I almost lost it. I wanted to throttle him. What was he doing in the hallway talking to who the fuck ever? Why wasn't he with my girl?

Luckily one of the residents interceded and explained what was going on to me.

Jade was having an ectopic pregnancy. Which is dangerous and her life was at risk. The baby, our baby, would never survive in the fallopian tube, so they had to perform the surgery to remove it. She could have children in the future if she wanted.

She wanted me there before they took her in for surgery, but they had to make a quick decision. Waiting was not a good idea.

The surgery went well.

There were no complications.

She was in recovery.

She would be moved into a regular room in an hour or so, and I could wait for her there. Which I didn't do. Because I had to make a stop first.

"HEY, LITTLE STAR."

"Hey."

"How ya feeling?"

"Like a Mack truck ran me over and then backed up again."

"Well you look goddamn amazing."

"You're a liar, Camden King."

"Yeah, I am." I smirk.

She winces in pain after giggling.

"Stop laughing if it hurts," I tell her.

"Stop making me laugh."

"I spilled your green juice all over Sansom Street, so you're shit out of luck."

"Thanks a lot. I was thirsty."

"Who told you to go into surgery while I was getting it?"

"I'm sorry, Cam. You can say it if you want."

"Say what?"

"I told you so. I was pregnant."

"That's not how I wanted to be right."

"Yeah."

"We'll try for real when we're ready."

"Sure, when we're ready, but in the meantime I think we're going to have to use condoms."

"We're not fucking ever again if this is what can happen. You scared the fuck out of me."

She winces again.

"I told you not to make me laugh."

"What's so funny about that?"

"You and I never having sex again?"

"I won't if it means putting you at risk."

"At risk of dying from dick withdrawal."

Now I laugh out loud.

"Ok, maybe we'll just give it a few weeks."

I bend over and kiss her forehead.

"I give a good blow job. That should hold you over."

"Jade."

"Hmmm?"

"What am I going to do with you?"

"Everything."

I kiss her carefully on the mouth this time.

"Get better soon. We have a wedding to go to."

"Damn, did they set a date while I was in surgery?"

"Something like that. It's the third Saturday in August."

"Sweet."

"And now..." I bend down on my knees and lean over on her bedside. "We need to set our own date."

I pull a small red box out of my pocket. While Jade was

in recovery I took an Uber a few blocks over to Jeweler's Row and picked out a ring. A princess cut diamond, with the highest clarity I could find, size five.

"Marry me."

Jade's mouth spreads in a smile. With IV's running through her veins, she lifts her slender arm and places her hand on the side of my head. Tracing her thumb across my eyebrow.

"Yes."

"I love you so much, lima bean."

"I love you too."

I lift up and kiss her gingerly. Only giving her a smidgen of tongue. I mean she did just get out of surgery. I don't want to hurt her.

"Cam?"

Oh crap, did I just hurt her?

"Yes, baby."

"I think we both need a breath mint."

I laugh out loud again.

My girl is going to be just fine.

CUTTER

AUGUST

I think my bride is secretly a sadist. It was her bright idea to house the groomsmen on one side of Roman's yacht and the bridesmaids on the other for the last twenty-four hours. Every man on this boat despises her. The women probably do too, although they'd probably never admit it.

Roman, Elizabeth, and baby Masterson graciously lent us the yacht for our impromptu summer wedding. We invited a little over one hundred and fifty guests and one-hundred and twenty-two were able to make it.

I haven't had my hands on Sloan in close to a day and a half, and I'm itching to see her.

To marry her.

To fuck her.

To love her.

"You'll see her soon, brother. You want a drink?" Camden offers me a highball of scotch and water.

"Then I'll taste like scotch when I kiss her."

"You taste like scotch all the damn time. What does it matter? She's going to marry you regardless."

Stone snickers over on the side.

"What are you laughing at?" I ask.

Over the last few months we have gotten to know our brother a lot better, and so I feel more comfortable giving him shit in the same way I give it to Camden.

"You can't go one day without her?"

"When's the last time you didn't sleep next to your woman?"

"Last fucking night thanks to your bride."

"Ooh, someone sounds like they're a little pissed as well!" I tease.

"When are you going to make an honest woman out of that sweet girl?" Camden asks.

"After my probation is over."

"That's a long ass time," Roman interjects. "You think she's going to wait for you that long?"

Stone cuts his eyes at Roman. Those two are slowly but surely beginning to understand each other.

"She'll wait."

"Better hope so. Tiny is a keeper."

"Her name is Ariana, asshole."

Okay, maybe Rome and Stone have a little work left to do. They'll get there.

"Excuse me." Someone knocks then pops their head into my cabin. "Hello?"

It's my brother's computer geek friend, Samar.

"Hey, Samar. Come on in."

"Hey, there. I just wanted to tell you that everyone is seated and the officiant is ready."

"Thanks, man. How's your woman liking the ship?" Camden asks.

"She loves it. Thanks for inviting us and thank you for everything you did to get her over here from India. You guys are the best."

"No thanks necessary, Samar. Glad you're on board. I mean that literally and figuratively," I say.

We all laugh.

"Well, brother. Let's go get you married."

I eagerly throw on my jacket and take a last minute swig of Roman's very expensive scotch. I'm ready.

"Let's do it!"

SLOAN

I smell river water and roses and freesias. I see small waves and seagulls and love around me.

The gauze fabric of my dress ripples in the wind behind me as we sail towards nowhere.

I look to my left and my right and see the people I love. My sister, Elizabeth, Tiny, my old coworkers from the pharmaceutical company, some of my design clients (minus one Mr. *asshole* Prentis), and even both of my parents. Sitting next to each other with what I think are actual tears glistening in their eyes.

"And I, Cutter King, take thee, Sloan Pearson, to be my wedded wife, to have and to hold from this day forward, for better for worse, for richer for poorer, in sickness and in health, to love and cherish, till death us do part, according to God's holy ordinance."

"And I, Sloan Pearson, take thee, Cutter King, to be my wedded husband, to have and to hold from this day forward, for better for worse, for richer for poorer, in sickness and in health, to love and cherish, till death us do part, according to God's holy ordinance."

"And now the exchanging of the rings."

Cutter slides a custom designed diamond eternity band around my finger next to my engagement ring.

"With this ring I thee wed, with my body I thee worship, and with all my worldly goods I thee endow.

Then I slide a platinum and diamond band onto his left finger.

"With this ring I thee wed, with my body I thee worship, and with all my worldly goods I thee endow.

"In the name of the Father, and of the Son, and of the Holy Ghost. Amen. I now pronounce you both man and wife. Sir, you may kiss your bride."

Cutter wraps one of his hands around the side of my neck, claiming me in front of our entire ship full of guests, and kisses me with intense ownership and love.

"I love you, Mrs. King. I plan on making you a very happy woman for a very long time."

My knees almost wobble. His kiss overpowers me. I've missed him over these last two days. I can't believe we have to dance, and eat, and shake hands with over a hundred people, before he can be inside of me.

"I love you too, Mr. King."

"That's a good thing, because you're going to have a pretty long punishment for making me bunk on the other side of this ship last night."

"You promise?"

THE END

♡♡♡

If you enjoyed The King Brothers stories, please consider leaving a review for any or all of the books you enjoyed. They are very much appreciated and help readers find the books.

Next Up Is The Nighthawk Series...
START WITH GUNSLINGER!

THE NIGHTHAWK SERIES
lisa lang blakeney
GUNSLINGER
A Sports Romance
lisa lang blakeney
A SPORTS ROMANCE
lisa lang blakeney
DIESEL
A Sports Romance
HARD BODIES
SEXY NIGHTS
SWEET LOVE STORIES
www.LisaLangBlakeney.com

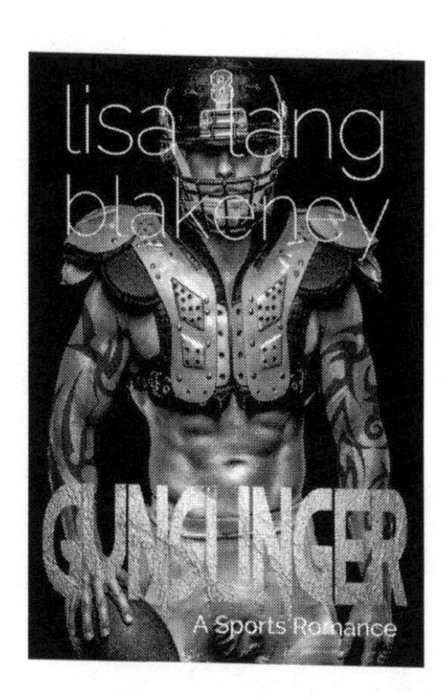

A hot, arrogant, NFL quarterback. A curvy, career driven, accountant. Can Saint and Sabrina put aside their differences and make this unique office romance work?

GUNSLINGER: A Quarterback Who Throws DEEP Risky Passes On The Field And Off...

I hate sports, and he is football royalty. I like quiet and predictable, but he's sex and swagger personified. I didn't particularly care for Saint Stevenson the first moment I laid eyes on him, but his warped brain seemed to process our initial meeting as foreplay.

I have a meticulous five year plan in place for myself and my career, but now this huge, cocky, self-absorbed quarterback who I've been assigned to at work is seriously f*cking it up.

He's the ultimate player on and off the field, and it doesn't make any sense that I'm falling hard and fast for the arrogant baller; but there doesn't seem to be anything about our love story that makes any sense at all.

Meet Alpha Saint Stevenson
The Nighthawk Series #1
Standalone Sports Romance
BUY NOW
Add To Goodreads

BONUS STUFF!

Want access to all my bonus stuff? Read deleted scenes, character interviews, and extended epilogues for all of my releases when you visit the **Romance Ninja Room**.

CLICK FOR EXCLUSIVE ACCESS
http://lisalangblakeney.com/private-ninja-room/

WHERE YOU CAN FIND ME

WHERE YOU CAN FIND ME

1. I have a VIP mailing list. I only send free books, new release, sale or special giveaway information to this group. No spam. You can join here: http://LisaLangBlakeney.com/VIP .

2. I have a private Fan & Readers Group also known as my "Ninjas" a.k.a. "Alpha Romance Warriors" where I share all things new going on, teasers, yummy pics, and just chit chat. It's a closed group for ages 18+ and over, and what we post won't show on your public feed: https://www.facebook.com/groups/romanceninjas/

3. I have a special ARC team. If you enjoy my books and would like a free advanced reader copy of my next book in exchange for an honest review on release day, then feel free to apply. There are only a certain number of slots and participation is strictly enforced, but I'd love to have you:)

To apply, please go here: http://lisalangblakeney.com/arc-reviewers/

BOOK LIST

The Masterson Series

Masterson

Masterson Unleashed

Masterson In Love

Joseph Loves Juliette

The King Brothers Series

Claimed

Indebted

Broken

Promised

The Nighthawk Series

Gunslinger

Wolf

Diesel

The Valencia Mafia Series

Rum Runners

ACKNOWLEDGMENTS

Special shout out to beta reader and super ninja **Jessie Lynn,** and a big thank you to every single reader who has taken a chance on me and my alphas. You all are awesome! Please keep reading. My alphas demand it!

ABOUT THE AUTHOR

Lisa Lang Blakeney is an international bestselling author of contemporary romance sold in more than 28 countries. Worried that her fellow PTO moms might disapprove, she wrote and published her steamy debut novel Masterson under a different title and pen name in August of 2015.

Thanks to strong reader support of her alpha male character, Roman Masterson, she was encouraged to continue with the series and published the entire Masterson Trilogy the following year. She hasn't looked back since and continues to write novels featuring strong alpha men and the smart women they seek to claim.

A romance junkie for sure, you can find Lisa watching a romantic comedy, reading a romance novel, or writing one of her own most days of the week. If she's not doing that, she's outside in the garden tending to her roses.

Lisa is the wife of one alpha (whom she met in college), mother to four girls, and two labradoodles. Get news on releases, sales and giveaways when you become one of Lisa's VIP readers at : http://LisaLangBlakeney.com/VIP

Made in the USA
Columbia, SC
15 November 2020

24643970R00100